the PALOMINO ☆ PONY RUNS FREE

Look out for:

the
PaLOMiNO
✿PONY
COMES
HOME

the
PaLOMiNO
✿PONY
WINS
THROUGH

the
PaLOMiNO
✿PONY
RIDES
OUT

the PALOMINO PONY RUNS FREE

OLIVIA TUFFIN

nosy
crow

With special thanks to Michelle Misra

First published 2015 by Nosy Crow Ltd
The Crow's Nest, 10a Lant Street
London SE1 1QR
www.nosycrow.com

ISBN: 978 0 85763 444 3

Nosy Crow and associated logos are trademarks
and/or registered trademarks of Nosy Crow Ltd

Text © Olivia Tuffin 2015

The right of Olivia Tuffin to be identified as the author has been asserted.

A CIP catalogue record for this book is available from the British Library.

Printed and bound in the UK by Clays Ltd, St Ives Plc.
Typeset by Tiger Media Ltd, Bishops Stortford, Hertfordshire

Papers used by Nosy Crow are made from wood grown in
sustainable forests.

1 3 5 7 9 8 6 4 2

For little Grace,
who's pony mad like me!
O.T.

PROLOGUE

The boy placed a comforting hand on the neck of his dark brown mare as he guided her carefully down the ramp. Three gorgeous ponies caught his eye as he glanced around the pretty cobbled yard; they were gazing at the new arrivals with keen interest. His first impression was that this was a really well-kept, happy yard and he was sure they would be fine here – it was just so different to home.

Clicking his tongue, he led the mare into a box and began settling her in. What would the other people be like? He had heard a bit about the teenage girl who had a pony here, but other than that, he didn't know much. Thinking of home again, he pressed his face against his pony's neck as she snuffled his hand, comforting him. He sighed heavily.

This was it. He had one last shot, one last chance to succeed. He didn't know if it would work, but he needed to try his very best for his pony's sake. Gathering his thoughts, the boy pulled on his baseball cap, straightened up and stepped out into the sunlight, ready to meet the yard owner. Looking back at his pony, he took a deep breath. It was important that he created the right impression and did not let his mask slip even once. He had to do this for his pony – to repay all that she had done for his family over the years.

CHAPTER ONE

"Georgia? Are you listening?"

Georgia's friend, Dan, gave her a nudge as the teacher walked over and stood in front of them.

"Sorry, could you repeat the question?" Georgia asked, trying to focus on the whiteboard at the front of the class. She was experiencing it again – an uncontrollable, tummy-churning rush of nerves that had arrived totally out of the blue in the middle of a history lesson. Georgia clenched and unclenched her clammy hands. She felt quite lightheaded as she pushed aside an unruly blonde curl and looked apologetically up at the teacher.

Dan shot her a sympathetic look, but luckily Miss Hayes had given up waiting for her answer and had turned her attention back to the whiteboard. Georgia tried to concentrate, but the noise of the classroom had become nothing more than a background hum now. As she closed her eyes, all Georgia could see were the bright lights of the arena at the Horse of the Year Show, and all she could feel was serious panic!

Once the pure shock and elation at qualifying for the Show had worn off, Georgia had started to feel the pressure of competing at such a level. From that point on, all eyes had been firmly on her and Georgia had begun to have doubts about whether she and Lily deserved their place at the

the PaLOMiNO ☆PONY

Horse of the Year Show. The pretty palomino had caught everyone's eye as soon as they'd started competing, but as Georgia was new on the circuit no one had viewed them as serious contenders until now. Georgia had only been riding Lily since last summer, and even though they were a brilliant pairing she couldn't help but feel nervous. And if she felt like this with several weeks still to go, what was she going to be like on the actual day?

Georgia let out a shuddering breath, which caused Miss Hayes to look around at her again.

"I–I'm sorry. I'm not feeling well," Georgia stammered. "May I go to the bathroom?"

☆ ☆ ☆

"What was all that about?" Dan asked as he caught up with Georgia after school, jogging beside her as she hurried down the corridor and out to the bus. "Are you OK? What's the huge rush?"

"I just want to get to the stables, all right?"

snapped Georgia. "To see Lily." As Dan fell into step beside her, Georgia took a deep breath and imagined resting her head against the palomino pony's neck. She knew that burying her face in Lily's creamy mane and breathing in her sweet horsey scent would make her feel so much better!

"Is it the Horse of the Year Show again?" Dan raised an eyebrow. "You know Georgia, you don't *have* to compete. Not if it's bothering you this much. No one would mind, especially not Melanie!"

"Do you really think so?" Georgia considered this as she thought about Melanie, the owner of Redgrove Farm, where Lily was kept. Melanie had done so much for her – she had saved the little palomino pony by buying her, for starters – and then she had given her to Georgia on loan.

"Yes, I do," Dan replied. "You just have to do what's best for you."

6

Georgia knew that he was right. But it had always been a dream of hers to compete in the Horse of the Year Show, and then to carry on year after year as a professional show rider. But now that it was within her reach, the thought of taking part completely terrified her!

"Oh, I don't know," she said, shaking her head as the school bus pulled up outside the gates to Redgrove Farm and the swing doors brushed open. "I'll call you later, Dan, OK?"

"Sure." Dan waved and Georgia jumped down, making her way up the drive and past the tennis court and paddocks. Redgrove Farm was a large modern house with stables attached. It had everything that you could possibly want – even a swimming pool! Georgia felt so lucky that she was allowed to come and ride here whenever she wanted. She lived with her mum in the village, but she came to the stables every day.

As Georgia made her way into the yard, a few of Melanie's bantam chickens were scratching around the edge of the hay barn, searching for stray pony nuts. There was a note pinned to the board in the feed room.

Hey G, I'm out at a Pony Club meeting. Can you come and see me when you get back from your ride?

The writing was Melanie's and she'd added a little smiley face. Georgia thought that Melanie probably wanted to talk about Lily's training routine for the run-up to the Show. A shiver ran down Georgia's spine again and she had to shake herself. She was just here to hack out on Lily this evening. No pressure!

Picking up the little mare's tack – a simple snaffle bridle and soft suede saddle – she made her way to the fields. Callie and Wilson – Melanie's other ponies – were already waiting by the gate. Wilson, a dark brown thoroughbred cross, was wearing a lightweight rug to keep him warm but Callie was unclad, her hardy Exmoor coat protecting her from the chilly breeze. The sky was still as blue as it had been in the summer but there was a definite nip in the air. Georgia wrapped her jacket a little tighter round her.

"Looking for a treat again, Callie?" She chuckled as Callie's soft nose brushed against her hand. Georgia pulled a Polo mint from her pocket and gave it to her. She looked over the Exmoor's back to see Lily hanging back, behind Wilson.

Georgia felt all her troubles wash away as the palomino whickered a greeting and gently pushed her way through the other ponies. Seeing Lily always made Georgia smile! The little Welsh pony had never looked better. Her champagne coat shone brightly and her creamy mane was lustrous and soft, brushed by Georgia every day until it was as smooth as silk. Her muscles were clearly defined beneath her coat, but Lily was slim and elegant and her delicate neck arched as she nuzzled Georgia, gently breathing on her face. You'd never know that she had foaled last year – a little colt called Secret who had gone to live at Josephine Smalley's show yard, up the road. Georgia had worked her gently since Secret was weaned, and Lily looked amazing!

"Let's get you tacked up," said Georgia, slipping the bridle over Lily's head and sliding the saddle down her back. If only Eric, Lily's breeder, could see her now. Georgia had heard that he had been in and out of hospital, so she hoped he was OK. She had sent him Lily's qualifying rosette in the post with a letter but hadn't received a reply yet. Maybe his granddaughter, Jemma, had opened the letter. Georgia shuddered, remembering the events of the previous summer when she'd rescued Lily from the brutal girl. At least Jemma couldn't hurt Lily now, and with rumours circulating on the competition circuit about her cruel treatment of Lily, Jemma rarely showed her face at shows any more.

"Come on, my angel," Georgia whispered, leading Lily through the gate and gently pushing Wilson and Callie back. It was still light enough after school to have time for a decent ride and Georgia was able to squeeze in the all-important hill work to keep Lily fit.

Leading the palomino up to the yard, she tied her by the mounting block for a moment while she quickly changed into her old navy jodhs in the tack room. She tied her curly blonde hair back into a ponytail. Then, remembering Melanie's yard rules, she pulled on a high visibility jacket, just in case the sun started to set before she got back.

Swinging lightly into the saddle, she set off on one of her favourite rides. She meandered down the lane from the yard, then looped round the heath that fell between the stables and Dan's farm. On a clear day she could just make out the red brick building of the farm shop, and see Dan's black-and-white collie, Hattie, who liked to lie by the entrance catching the last rays of sunshine.

As Lily's long, fluid strides ate up the chalk path and she moved into a rolling, rhythmic canter, Georgia felt all her worries vanish. This was what riding was all about – being out and about and enjoying time with your pony. She concentrated on keeping her contact light and soft and her legs still in the stirrups, and time seemed to melt away.

But all too soon, it was time to head home. "Whoa lovely, whoa." Georgia soothed the little mare back to a walk, letting her have her head so she could warm-down after her hill work. Lily stretched her long, elegant neck and gave a happy snort. Georgia laughed and patted her, thinking again how lucky she was to have the palomino pony.

She was so deep in thought that she almost didn't hear the heavy thud of hooves until another horse was suddenly bearing down on them.

Lily gave a startled squeal, leaping into the air as a sleek dark brown pony overtook her at a fast canter.

"Wotcha!" The rider laughed as he hurtled past, turning sideways to grin at Georgia and flashing white, straight teeth. He was wearing a dark green baseball cap instead of a riding hat and a blue zip up jacket with motifs emblazoned on it.

"Hey – watch it!" Georgia cried, unnerved as Lily plunged forwards and half-reared. Everyone knew you should wear a hard hat and it was an unwritten rule that you should be careful not to pass other ponies at speed when you hacked out! The rider and his dark brown pony continued on around the bend before disappearing from view, leaving Lily crabbing sideways.

Georgia was furious. Soothing Lily, she patted her neck and walked her forwards in the direction of Redgrove, outwardly calm but seething with anger inside. Whoever that rider was, he could have caused Lily to bolt or fall. Georgia shuddered to think of the palomino crashing to the ground and hurting herself. Their perfect evening ride had been ruined by that arrogant boy and his pony – and just when Georgia had started to relax and forget her worries. What an idiot!

CHAPTER TWO

Georgia was still muttering crossly to herself as she untacked Lily and rugged her up for the night. The little mare was calm again now and stood quietly, enjoying the attention, closing her white-lashed eyes. Carefully, Georgia wiped the pony's face with a cloth. "It's just lucky you're so trusting now," she murmured as she finished her grooming routine. "That stupid rider could have really unnerved you!"

"Georgia!"

Melanie's voice cut across her thoughts and she whirled round to see the owner of Redgrove striding across the yard, a terrier at each heel. Kind, caring and a brilliant rider, Melanie was Georgia's absolute role model, and had taught her everything she knew about ponies.

"Hello Georgia, hello Lily…" Melanie paused to stroke the little mare. "Goodness she's looking well, isn't she? Anyway, G, I'm glad I caught you. I nearly didn't get out of that Pony Club meeting alive – you know what Janey's like, planning rallies left, right and centre!"

Georgia chuckled. She loved Janey, the Pony Club instructor, but she could be fierce, and she liked to talk – a lot!

"Anyway," Melanie continued, raking her hands through her dark hair and securing it with

16

a tortoiseshell clip. "There's something that I meant to tell you yesterday … but it all happened so fast, and it was a bit last-minute. You remember Sara, who used to live in the village?" Georgia vaguely recalled one of Melanie's horsey friends and nodded.

"She's the one who had Sophie to stay for a while when she was doing her university placement last term," Melanie went on. "So I owe her a favour – and she's asked if we can have her nephew and his pony here in the run up to the Horse of the Year Show – just to help him keep focused. He qualified like you did, but as a working hunter jumper, not a flat show rider."

"Really?" At the mention of the Horse of the Year Show, Georgia was immediately interested!

"Yes, he's come to train with Janey," Melanie continued, stroking Lily. "He used to be in the Round Barrow Pony Club. I said we had a spare stable."

Georgia's interest was definitely piqued. A new livery, *and* one that was also going to the Horse of the Year Show! Georgia hadn't been on the competition scene for long and so she didn't know anyone else who had qualified. Although Dan and Emma – her other best friend – shared her excitement, it was hard for them to understand the enormous scale of the event, so it would be great to have someone to talk to about it. She could ask him how he was dealing with his nerves. Or maybe he could even give her some help with her jumping. Although Lily was an excellent jumper, Georgia always felt more comfortable doing flatwork.

"So, what do you think?" asked Melanie.

"Sounds great," said Georgia. "We can compare notes and it'll be someone to ride out with as well." She grinned enthusiastically.

"When does he arrive?"

"Well…" Melanie's answer was cut short by a shrill whinny from Callie as the yard gates opened and a horse and rider clattered over the cobbled floor. "He's actually already here!"

Georgia looked up and let out a gasp. Trotting towards her was the dark brown mare from earlier – the one that had nearly run them down out on the heath. Georgia's eyes narrowed as Melanie continued talking.

"I know you'll get along brilliantly," she was saying. "You're both as pony crazy as each other! Georgia meet Will. Will – Georgia! Oh, and Will's pony, Santa." Pausing, Melanie gave a sigh of exasperation. "Sorry, Will, I don't mean to nag on your first day, but when you ride here, hard hats on, please."

The rider, Will, had now dismounted and removed his baseball cap, revealing thick dark hair.

"Sure, Melanie. Sorry about that," he apologised, speaking with a polished accent. "My brother's habit." Smiling at Georgia, he stuck out a hand to greet her.

"We've met," Georgia said icily, reluctantly shaking his hand as Melanie raised an eyebrow in surprise. "Out on the ridgeback … when you nearly ran us over."

"Ah, that was you! Sorry about that!" Will chuckled, not sounding sorry at all. "Melanie did tell me you rode flat in the show ring; I guess us jumpers are just used to cutting across each other in the warm up!"

"OK, guys, I'll leave you to get to know each other," Melanie said, glancing at her watch. "I need to get on and cook supper." And with that she headed back into the house.

"You could have caused an accident back there!" Georgia burst out once Melanie was out of earshot, struggling to stay calm. Then she took a deep breath – after all, this was a family friend of Melanie's and he would be staying here until the championships, so she had to try to be polite! "Next time you ride on the heath just slow down if you see another horse, OK?" She knew she sounded patronising but she still couldn't believe how badly Will had behaved earlier.

"Yessir!" Will clicked his heels together and pretended to salute.

Ugh, he was worse than Harry Blake, one of the few boys in the Round Barrow Pony Club, and Harry was annoying enough! Giving Will an icy smile, Georgia turned her attention back to Lily, who was gazing at the new arrival. She whinnied gently and the dark brown mare whickered back, a kind expression in her eyes. Georgia had to admit that Will's pony was a beauty, even if *he* was a complete idiot. The brown mare had some native in her, New Forest perhaps, but also some Arab lines or thoroughbred as well, and she was obviously bred for speed and jumping.

Concentrating on brushing Lily down, Georgia tried to stifle her bad mood. They'd got off on the wrong foot, but maybe he wouldn't turn out to be so bad after all!

CHAPTER THREE

"He's awful, totally awful!"

It was a couple of days later at school, and Georgia was complaining loudly to Emma and Dan, stabbing at her yoghurt pot with her spoon in frustration.

Emma raised an eyebrow, looking up from her book. She hadn't met Will yet, but had heard plenty about the new arrival already! "Is he really *so* bad?" she said mildly. "I can't imagine Melanie letting anyone that terrible stable at Redgrove."

Georgia snorted and shook her head. "You have no idea what he's like!"

Still, she wasn't *really* sure what Emma would make of Will. She'd probably think he was OK! After all, Will was totally charming towards everyone else – Melanie, her husband Simon... Even Georgia's mum had laughed along at his stupid jokes when she'd come to the stables with her weekly bag of carrots for Lily. But Will was always messing around, winding Georgia up and spoiling her enjoyment of the yard. And he was arrogant too, going on about the number of classes he'd won, and how he rode at the highest level. Georgia knew she had to be polite as he was Melanie's guest and livery, and it certainly wasn't up to her who stabled at Redgrove. But it was hard, particularly when he kept referring to her beloved Lily as Barbie's pony!

"So what's he like to look at then?" Emma asked.

Georgia groaned. "Oh Em, is that all you can think about? He's got dark hair, kind of wavy, and er ... blue eyes, I think."

"So you mean he's good-looking?" Emma raised an eyebrow.

"No ... well, yes," Georgia said grudgingly. "I suppose so – if you like that kind of thing."

Emma grinned, but Georgia huffed and turned away. She really couldn't stand Will. And yet, she had to admit that he was dedicated to his horse. He was totally driven – more so than any rider Georgia had ever met. She was used to the older members of the Round Barrow, who, with the odd exception, mostly only rode for the social side of the club. And there were others who only rode because their parents wanted them to. But Will was completely different. When he wasn't jumping huge fences and complicated-looking grids in Melanie's school, he was out running – sometimes by five in the morning, according to Melanie. Despite his jokes and messing around, there was a steely determination to the boy.

"Come on, G, he's OK," Dan chimed in. He was sitting on the other side of her and until now had been quietly flicking through a tractor catalogue and eating his sandwiches. Dan had been pleased to find that the new livery was a boy about his age, and had even kicked a football about with him at Redgrove the previous night, while Georgia swept the yard.

"Dan!" Georgia was hurt. "You're meant to be on my side!"

"Oh, come off it, Georgia." Dan looked a bit grumpy. "I know you're stressed at the moment, but give it a rest!"

Georgia swallowed hard as tears pricked her

eyes. She knew her worries over the Horse of the Year Show were getting to her but, until now, she hadn't realised that she'd been annoying her friends as well.

"Hey – it's all right, G." Dan softened, as he saw her looking upset. "I'm not having a go at you. I'm just saying that we know Will got off to a bad start with you when he upset Lily that time on the heath, but honestly, he's OK! You should give him a chance."

"OK," Georgia mumbled. She suddenly felt a bit silly for going on about Will so much. She smiled weakly at Dan. "I should be concentrating entirely on Lily, anyway." She took a deep breath. "I promise to give Will a break."

☆ ☆ ☆

Later that afternoon, after school, Georgia remembered her promise and attempted to make conversation with Will while they were grooming their ponies. Santa stood quietly on one side of the tie bar, with Lily on the other. The dark brown mare lazily swished her tail, and the palomino arched her neck over towards her new friend. The two ponies had similar temperaments – both kind and willing – and, unlike Will and Georgia, had adored each other at first sight.

"So…" Georgia tried to think of something to talk about. "Aren't you missing loads of school to train here?" she asked eventually, thinking about all the lessons she'd had that day.

"No," Will chuckled. "I'm home-schooled. I'm a G&T, you see!" Laughing at Georgia's puzzled expression he carried on. "G&T – it stands for gifted and talented. My brother home-schools me so that I can concentrate on my jumping."

"Oh, right." Georgia was amazed – she had never met anyone her age that didn't have to attend school. Will must be really good at competing if that was the case! She cleared her throat. "So does your brother ride as well?" she asked.

Will laughed loudly, making Georgia blush. "Yes!" he chortled. "Haven't you heard of him? Jasper Bowen?"

Georgia thought hard. She tried to keep up with who-was-who on the showing scene, but still didn't really know that many people – only Melanie and the riders from Josephine Smalley's yard where Secret now lived. It was easier to keep up with if you were from a horsey family, which she wasn't, and she'd only been riding competitively for a year. "No, I'm afraid I haven't heard of him," she said carefully, not wanting to offend Will in case his brother really was very well-known.

"Well, he's *only* one of the most famous show riders around," Will said, sounding boastful. "He's a brilliant rider, has an amazing yard, top ponies, and a super-luxurious horsebox, and he's still only twenty-five. He's sponsored by Diamond Horses. *Pur-lease* tell me you've heard of them at least?"

Georgia looked blank.

Will laughed. "Man, you really are new to the competition world, aren't you? Diamond Horses? You know – they make the jackets that *every* cool show rider wears if they know what's what. They're huge. Everyone wants to be sponsored by them!"

"Oh, right," Georgia said, thinking of her old but perfectly smart tweed jacket that used to belong to Sophie.

"He usually trains me," Will went on. "Only he can't at the moment. That's why I'm here – Janey used to teach us at Pony Club," Will continued, "so she seemed the most obvious person to stand in."

"Oh, right," Georgia said again. She sounded

so young and amateurish compared to Will. She asked, curiously, "Why can't your brother train you?" then immediately wished she hadn't as Will's face clouded over.

"He just can't, not at the moment," he said shortly, looking away.

"Oh, OK," Georgia replied, not knowing what to say to that. This conversation hadn't exactly gone the way she had hoped!

The two of them continued to groom their ponies in awkward silence for a while. After a few minutes, Georgia decided to try again. "Santa's so lovely," she said, reaching out a hand to stroke Will's pony on her soft muzzle.

"Yeah, she is, isn't she?" Softening, Will smiled, patting the dark brown mare on her neck. "She's the best. She's been in our family for years. My brother used to ride her." He paused, and the tone of his voice suddenly changed again. "It's just a shame…" He glanced quickly at Georgia before looking away again. "Oh, never mind."

"Never mind what?" Georgia had detected a note of sadness in Will's normally upbeat, arrogant voice. She looked at him. He was still stroking Santa's dark brown neck, but now there was a serious expression on his face that had replaced his usual carefree one.

"Nothing," he said quickly. The familiar teasing tone had returned to his voice. "So how do you rate Barbie's pony's chances in the ring anyway?"

Georgia frowned. Lily was *not* a Barbie pony, and she was tired of Will calling her that! She opened her mouth to defend Lily, but he had already walked off. She thought hard. What had Will been about to say? And why was he so defensive about his brother? Clearly something was going on, and Georgia was determined to get to the bottom of it…

CHAPTER FOUR

Later that day, Georgia was riding Lily in the bottom paddock and working on her individual show, when she noticed Will lounging against the post and rail fence, baseball cap pulled over his eyes, intently watching her school. He was holding Santa's reins in his hands and the little brown mare was also watching with interest. Already feeling nervous, Georgia nudged Lily into a trot and then a canter, hoping to work on her extension down the long side. She was concentrating so hard, though, that she fluffed the lead and put Lily on to the wrong leg. Bringing her back to a trot she corrected her mistake, feeling flustered. As she passed Will, he called out to her and she slowed down.

"Here," he said. "Try that again. You can't make those sorts of mistakes at the Horse of the Year."

"Yes, I know," Georgia said, embarrassed but also annoyed at Will for pointing out the obvious. Rounding the corner, she tried her canter-lead again, but feeling Will's eyes burning into her, she made the same mistake. With Wilson she could perhaps have got away with it as he was such a old hand, but Lily was so much more sensitive and responsive to even the most subtle of aids that Georgia had to ride her perfectly. Again, she corrected her mistake, her cheeks flushed.

"You need to work on that," Will called out again. He had mounted Santa and they were warming up in the paddock now. "Watch this," he said as he and the brown mare passed Georgia. Nudging her into a trot, they took up the correct lead and then proceeded to canter the most perfect figure-of-eight, even throwing in a spectacular flying change across the diagonal. Santa moved like a ballet dancer, her hooves flicking up extravagantly, perfectly on the bit. "Like that," Will said as he slowed his mare down, patting her on the neck. "You have to up your game a bit if you're riding at the top."

"Right," Georgia said, completely taken aback. Will didn't mince his words, and her cheeks stung with mortification as he continued, seemingly oblivious to her upset.

"My brother would love a pony like Lily," he said. "He'd get her going like a champion, you'd see. Let me know if Mel ever wants to sell her, won't you?"

That was the final straw for Georgia. She turned Lily back towards the stables, fuming, but also feeling totally useless. There were no two ways about it – Will had successfully ruined her afternoon!

☆ ☆ ☆

Early next morning, Georgia decided to cycle to Redgrove before catching the school bus. If she'd finished all of her homework and gone to bed early enough, her mum usually let her go to the stables before the bus arrived to pick her up. Normally Melanie turned Lily out for her in the morning, but that day Georgia planned to give Lily an extra groom and muck her out so she could train her that evening instead, and hopefully avoid Will. She had slept really badly after her schooling session – aware she was nowhere near his league and certainly not feeling good enough to compete at the Horse of the Year Show. She could feel her confidence shrinking every day. Will was right, she couldn't make those mistakes, but the way he'd spoken to her had made Georgia feel awful.

The mornings were still light but there was a thick fog enveloping the valley as she cycled down the hill towards the yard, and she was grateful for her reflective coat and bike lights. Pip, her little black-and-white spaniel, excited to be getting an extra walk, barked excitedly as she ran next to the bike. The lights were on in the yard as she propped her bike up against the stone pillars. Santa's rug was hanging over her open stable door, her head collar still attached to the tie ring. Will must be out riding. Georgia sighed and, glancing at her watch, saw that it was only six thirty am.

Wow, she thought, *that's very early to be out training!* Glancing around the corner, she focused on the outdoor school, where Will was cantering a circle on the dark brown mare. There was a grid set up on the long side made up of Melanie's rustic poles, ending in a huge jump that was at least one metre fifteen, huge, upright and imposing.

Swishing her glossy brown tail, Santa cantered towards the grid. Will's jaw was set in a hard line, and he didn't look happy. Santa jumped the first three lower jumps beautifully, but just as she approached the final upright, despite Will's quiet, concentrated riding she veered sharply to the left, half rearing and bolting away from the imposing jump. Will turned Santa back towards the grid. He hadn't seen Georgia yet. She was relieved to see that although Will carried a riding crop, he wasn't using it. It was clear that Santa wasn't being naughty – Georgia could tell instinctively that the little mare just didn't want to jump. Will briefly patted her neck, his jaw set tighter than ever.

38

Urging Santa on with his legs, once more he approached the preliminary jumps, and again, Santa flew over them beautifully, before tossing her elegant head and veering away from the final upright. This time, however, she turned so sharply, almost rearing vertically, that it unseated Will and he fell heavily on to his side. Sitting for a moment on the damp sand of the school, he then buried his face in his hands and let out a shout of frustration. Or was it upset? Georgia couldn't tell. Without thinking, she ran into the arena and caught Santa, who looked crestfallen, her head hanging.

"There girl, there..." Stroking Santa's glossy neck, Georgia attempted to soothe her.

Will hauled himself up and limped over towards Georgia, his eyes glistening, and she glanced away, embarrassed. "Are you OK?" she whispered, concentrating hard on Santa's mane instead of Will.

"Fine." His reply was abrupt, cutting. He took Santa's reins and quickly led her back to the yard, where he carefully checked her legs. Feeling awkward, Georgia walked behind. She didn't want him to think she was following him but she still needed to turn Lily out.

The palomino whickered when Georgia came into the yard, her lovely amber eyes registering interest at all this activity so early in the morning. Evidently thinking she might be going to a show, she shuffled excitedly from side to side, nibbling at the bolt on the door. Georgia smiled and put Lily's head collar on before leading her out into the paddock.

Will was untacking Santa by the time she returned. Worried in case he had hurt himself when he fell, Georgia walked quietly over to his stable where Santa was now resting a leg.

"Will?" Georgia hesitated. "Are you OK? Did you hurt yourself?"

"I'm fine." Will's voice took on its usual, arrogant tone again, all the shakiness from earlier gone. "Just an off day, that's all. I didn't think anyone would be around. I expect you distracted Santa – spooked her when you came round the corner."

"Oh, I…" Georgia blushed. She didn't think that had been the case – after all, Santa was a top jumping pony, so was surely used to crowds. She hadn't looked distracted either. She had looked as though she genuinely didn't want to jump the heights Will was attempting! But there was something about Will's face that made her keep her mouth closed. "OK," she said quietly. "I'll let you know next time I'm here really early."

Heading towards Wilson's stable, ready to put him in the field with Lily, Georgia shook her head.

That was really strange. Why was Will over-facing his pony, and why was he putting on that front? Perhaps the pressures of the big show were getting to him after all…

CHAPTER FIVE

"Melanie?"

It was later that week, and Georgia was sitting at the big wooden kitchen table at Redgrove, cleaning tack. She had been thinking about Will for the past few days – the way he had spoken the evening they'd been schooling their ponies, and what she had seen when he'd been jumping Santa early in the morning.

Melanie looked up from her computer. "Yes?" She adjusted the glasses she wore for reading and pushed her chair back.

"Is everything..." Georgia wasn't quite sure what she wanted to say, and felt guilty for prying. "I mean, do you think everything's OK with Will? You know – considering how hard he's pushing Santa, and himself?"

"Hmm." Melanie looked thoughtful. "I have wondered about that. Will's brother does get results from their horses and they're good at what they do. I remember that from when they were in Pony Club. If I thought that Santa's welfare was being compromised, I would say something. She's a lovely pony, and Will is a great rider. I think it's just that they do things differently to us, that's all." She smiled at Georgia. "Anyway, let's think about your show with Lily. How are you feeling?"

the PALOMINO ☆PONY

"OK…" Georgia crossed her fingers under the kitchen table, hoping Melanie wouldn't notice the colour draining from her face. Once again, she wished that she had confessed her fears about the championships earlier on. But with only three weeks to go, she was scared that it was too late now. Not only had Melanie and Sophie booked a hotel to stay in close to the showground, her mum was also going to take the day off and drive up early in the morning on the day of the Show. Georgia knew that it was an expense she couldn't easily spare. And of course Dan and Emma were coming too, having been given special permission to miss school. Everyone was really looking forward to it and she'd be letting them all down if she didn't go ahead.

She glanced out of the window, focusing on Lily who was grazing quietly next to the garden fence. No, Melanie couldn't know how she was

45

feeling. Instead she smiled brightly and tried to concentrate on the latest timetable for the Show day, swallowing her fears.

✩ ✩ ✩

"Ready, Georgia?" Mrs Black called her daughter from the bottom of the stairs the next evening, where she was waiting with Pip, car keys in hand.

"Coming, Mum." Georgia dragged a comb through her tangled blonde hair and hopped around on one foot, trying to locate her other trainer, which Pip had no doubt moved for her. Emma stood at the door, waiting, in new pink jeans and a black jumper, amused by her best friend's untidiness.

Georgia was taking a rare night off from the yard, but not from ponies! Instead, the two girls were attending a Pony Club rally, an unmounted one that was being held in a nearby village hall. Janey was so persuasive at getting members to attend, Georgia felt she couldn't say no, even though she would far rather be riding Lily. Melanie had encouraged Georgia to go as well because she had been involved in organising it. Mostly the unmounted rallies were quite interesting, with talks on everything from plaiting to dressage and visits by famous three-day-eventers. Tonight's talk was a bit less exciting – a first-aid course for pony clubbers. Georgia had been unlucky enough to fracture her wrist the previous summer and hoped never to have any more riding injuries. It had been awful not being able to ride for a few weeks. Still, perhaps she would learn something this evening.

As Georgia's mum drove the two girls towards the hall, she chatted to them about their day at school. Enthusiastically, Emma answered all of her questions but Georgia was tired, and didn't say much, causing her mum to glance sideways at her in concern.

"All OK, sweetheart?" she asked in a worried voice.

"Fine," Georgia responded, trying not to sound short. The last thing she needed was her mum questioning her about her nerves as well. "I'm just thinking about the championships."

Mrs Black glanced at her daughter again before continuing. "I hope you're thinking about school as well, Georgia. You know you have your big exams coming up."

"I know, Mum." Georgia knew she had to do well at school, or at least try her best. It was one of the conditions of having Lily on loan. She smiled as brightly as possible. "I promise that once the Horse of the Year Show is over, I won't think of anything but school."

Georgia knew that wasn't entirely true, but it

seemed to satisfy her mum. As they pulled up outside the hall, Harry Blake came into view. He was hanging around the entrance with a couple of the more popular girls. As they got out, he grinned and winked at Emma, who giggled in response.

"Oh, Emma!" Georgia muttered under her breath. He was such a flirt! She and Harry got on a little better since Georgia had ridden Wilson as part of the Round Barrow's Working Hunter Team, but even so, he was still a bit annoying. Tonight however, to her surprise, he wanted to chat to her, leaving his gaggle of admirers to come over.

"Hey, Georgia," he said in a friendly voice.

"Hi, Harry. How's Hector?" Georgia replied.

"Hector's fine," Harry grinned. "Still handsome, just like me!"

Georgia made a face and Harry laughed before continuing. "I hear you've got Will Bowen

49

staying at Redgrove?"

"Yes!" Georgia said in surprise. "Why – do you know him?"

"Know him?" Harry grinned. "No, not really, but my sister was in the same team at Pony Club with his brother, Jasper. He's a total hero! He's only like the best Working Hunter rider in the country…" He sounded a little awestruck as he continued. "You're so lucky having Will to stay with you. I bet he's just as cool!"

It didn't surprise Georgia that Harry would think that. Will did lead a pretty amazing life – not going to school, competing all over the country, riding brilliant ponies. Promising Harry that she would try to introduce him to Will, she and Emma went into the hall and took their seats.

The speaker for the evening was a friendly woman who was wearing jeans and a smart jumper. After introducing herself she began the talk, in which she showed various slides of falls and riding injuries. These caused the Pony Club members to gasp and wince! It was actually a lot more interesting than Georgia had expected. Not only were injuries covered, but emergencies as well. Georgia remembered the time at the Smalley show yard when she'd been helping out there and Secret had escaped. He was fine but one of the old stable girls, Lucy, had broken her leg. The whole situation had been really scary, and thinking about it still made Georgia shiver.

After the speaker had finished, the Pony Club members filed out of the hall, chatting among themselves. Emma looked a bit pale; she had never been very good with injuries, horsey or human. Georgia, who had listed a vet nurse as an alternative career if the show riding didn't work out, was thinking about what the speaker had said, trying to remember the important bits.

"Hope we never need to use any of that stuff!" Emma giggled nervously as they waited outside for Georgia's mum.

"Me too, Em," Georgia replied solemnly, agreeing with her friend. She had had more than enough drama in her life in the past year!

CHAPTER SIX

"Do you want me to come up to the yard with you tonight, Georgia?" Dan put his arm around her shoulder as they wandered between the history block and the arts centre the next afternoon at school. It was Careers Day and Georgia was heading to a talk. If any other boy had done that, Georgia would have pushed them away, but Dan was one of her best friends. There had been a bit more between them now and then and they had kissed a couple of times, but Dan knew that ponies were number one in Georgia's life and their relationship had slipped back into a relaxed friendship again lately.

"That would be great," said Georgia. "I've got a lesson with Janey at the stables this evening." She would be grateful for the support! Normally Melanie taught her, but she was busy that evening. Georgia had been trying to put off working on her show with Lily, worried it would only highlight how nervous she was, but Melanie had booked the lesson in so Georgia was just going to have to put on a brave face.

"OK – well, meet me by the bus stop after school then." Dan smiled warmly at Georgia, which made her feel slightly better. As long as Dan was with her, things always seemed all right. Pleased with the plan that they'd made, she headed over to the room where her next talk was being held.

The school's career lady was a brisk older woman who wore a high-necked blouse and glasses on the end of her nose. Consulting her notes, she gestured for Georgia to take a seat. "Hello, Georgia ... Georgia..."

"Black," Georgia finished for her. She felt nervous, but wasn't really sure why.

"So, Georgia Black, do you have any idea what you want to do on leaving school?" the lady asked, peering at her over her glasses.

"Oh, yes." Georgia nodded. "Have my own showing yard and bring on ponies to compete at the top."

"Goodness me." The woman beamed at her. "At least you know what you want to do. I used to showjump in my youth. So, are you riding at the moment?"

Georgia nodded again and told the woman

about her qualification for the Horse of the Year Show.

The careers advisor looked impressed. "Well, that's a good start then!" she said. "You must have nerves of steel!"

Georgia smiled weakly and swallowed hard. Nothing could be further from the truth. For a brief moment, she thought about pouring her heart out to the lady, who seemed kind, but she knew that would only make her dilemma real and then she'd have to do something about it. And she *did* want to compete ponies … it's just that her thoughts were so jumbled, it was difficult to know what she felt at the moment.

Instead, she tried to sound excited as the woman asked her more questions about her plans. She was getting quite good at covering up how she really felt these days.

There was no sign of anyone when Georgia and Dan got to the yard after school, but Santa was in her stable, picking quietly at a hay net. She hung her dark elegant head over the door when she saw Georgia and whickered as Lily came in to be brushed before her lesson.

"Where's Will?" Dan asked, picking up a brush and starting to comb out Lily's blonde hairs.

"I don't know." Georgia paused, scanning the yard. He was normally around. The fact Santa was in suggested that Will would probably be riding later, although hopefully not at the same time as Georgia – not after how she had ridden the last time he'd watched. Janey usually came over to train Will in the morning, when Georgia was at school. Will didn't seem to hack out any more, not since he had overtaken Georgia on the heath; he seemed to be concentrating mainly on his jumping.

"Getting on with him better now, are you?" Dan

asked casually, concentrating on brushing out Lily's mane.

Georgia frowned. "I suppose so, but I can't work him out. He has these funny mood changes. Why do you ask?"

But before Dan could reply, they were interrupted by the yard gates opening.

"Georgia, hi, ready to crack on?" Janey's raspy tones cut across the yard as she strode towards them, smartly dressed as always in a light down jacket, breeches and shiny long boots.

"Yes, sure." Georgia had just finished tacking Lily up, her simple snaffle bridle setting off her delicate head beautifully. Georgia still caught her breath sometimes when she saw Lily, and could hardly believe that she had been loaned such an exquisite mare, who was as sweet-natured as she was beautiful! Fastening her navy skull-cap and accepting a leg up from Dan, she went to the arena to join Janey, who was buttoning up her jacket against the slight chill.

"Right then." Janey sent Georgia round the arena in a workmanlike walk, admiring the palomino's fluid stride. Georgia was perched stiffly on top, her hands clenching the reins. Accustomed to Georgia's normal free way of riding, Janey frowned. "All OK, Georgia?" she called out.

Breathing deeply, Georgia tried to smile. "Fine!" she said, as brightly as possible, trying her best to relax. Lily also sensed her stiffness and flicked an ear back, as if to ask her young mistress what was wrong.

"OK," Janey said, obviously perplexed but pushing on with the lesson. She instructed Georgia to nudge Lily into a trot, and demonstrate the individual show that she and Melanie had been working on.

The show was designed for the judge to see

exactly how each pony could move, but without over-complicating things. Georgia had written down her floor plan and read it through every night before going to sleep, hoping it would become second nature to her. Now she trotted Lily round in a circle, imagining Janey was the judge. She crossed the diagonal. After that, was it left, or right rein? Georgia's mind went blank. She guided Lily round on the left rein, and then panicked and sent her right, resulting in a clumsy wrong leg canter.

"Easy girl." Steadying Lily and scratching her withers, Georgia apologized to the little mare, knowing that it was her fault, not Lily's. Again, Janey frowned. Georgia was still perched, her mouth set in a thin line. She guided Lily back across the diagonal. This was where she needed to extend Lily's trot, to really show off the palomino's movement.

Rushing, Georgia urged Lily on too quickly and, confused by her aids, the little mare broke into a choppy canter instead. The rest of the show didn't fare much better, and by the time Georgia gently halted Lily in front of Janey, her mouth was trembling and her eyes were glazed with unspilled tears. Reaching down and rubbing Lily's neck over and over, she felt awful. Poor Lily, it wasn't her fault.

"Georgia," Janey began gently. "What's the matter?"

Wiping her eyes on the back of her hand, Georgia tried to steady her voice before answering, "I'm sorry," she said, as brightly as possible. "I think I'm just having an off day, that's all."

"Really?" Janey didn't sound convinced. "Georgia, you do want to go to the Show, don't you?"

Georgia nodded hard, trying to convince her.

"Well, OK then." Janey had clearly decided not to push it. "Why don't you show me a couple of canter transitions and then go and cool off in the meadow." She patted Lily's neck. "If you're sure it's just an off day?" She let the question hang in the air.

The rest of the lesson stumbled on, ending with a correct canter transition at last, but only after an uncharacteristic flurry of wrong legs, with Georgia making the same mistakes as when Will had been watching. Georgia couldn't blame Lily one bit. She had given her the wrong aids and signals. She had ridden terribly. Lily was a sensitive mare who needed careful guidance, and knowing this, Georgia felt even worse.

Georgia thanked Janey for the lesson, who just nodded and patted Lily's neck in response. Then Georgia let the reins fall slack as she guided the little palomino towards the bottom meadow, ready to cool her off. Dan left his position at the side of the fence and hurried after her.

"Georgia?" Dan was more direct with his questioning than Janey had been. "You're clearly terrified about the Horse of the Year Show, and it's affecting your riding. Why are you putting yourself through it?" And stroking the palomino's neck he added as an afterthought, "And Lily, for that matter?"

"It's fine!" Georgia sounded much snappier than she meant to. "I'll be fine. As I said to Janey, it was just an off day, that's all. Everyone has them, even you. Or are you perfect all the time?!"

Instantly, she regretted what she had said. But how could she explain to Dan that she couldn't not ride at the championships? Not after all the time and help Melanie had invested in Lily. There was no way she could pull out now. Plus, didn't she want to be a successful show-pony rider when she had finished her GCSEs? There was no way any professional would give up because of a few nerves.

"All right." Dan let his arm fall from Lily's neck, a look of hurt crossing his open, honest face, making Georgia feel even worse.

"Dan…" she began, not knowing what to say, but knowing she needed to apologize.

"Don't worry, Georgia," Dan mumbled, not looking at her. "I just remembered I said I'd help Dad move some heifers tonight." Turning around, he started to walk back up the track towards the stables. "See you tomorrow at school." And with that, he was gone.

Feeling terrible, Georgia circled the meadow, letting Lily cool down and gathering her own thoughts. She knew she shouldn't have snapped at Dan like that, and promised herself she would text him as soon as she had untacked Lily. After all, Dan was right – she was terrified about the competition. As much as she had tried to tell herself that it would be no different from any other show, she knew that wasn't the case. But what would she regret more – pulling out now, or going as planned but having a miserable time in the run-up? Georgia wished she knew the answer…

CHAPTER SEVEN

Janey's blue Land Rover had gone by the time Georgia walked back into the yard with Lily. She had taken her time riding the circuit of the meadow, so that she could compose herself a little. The yard lights were on, casting a warm orange glow over Santa, Wilson and Callie who had been brought in for the night already. Callie gave an indignant whinny when she spotted Lily, as if to question where she had been. Glancing at the drive behind the house, Georgia saw that there was no sign of Melanie's car either, which was a relief. She felt sure that if anyone asked her how she was doing she would quite simply burst into tears, and then she'd have to confess everything. Then there would be no Horse of the Year Show for anyone directly connected with the stables and it would all be her fault.

However, there was a car there that Georgia didn't instantly recognize – a sleek navy saloon – and Will was emerging from Santa's stable, followed by a smartly dressed man. Both looked grim-faced and not in the mood for small talk, so Georgia hurried Lily into her stable and concentrated on untacking the palomino.

Will and the man were talking now in hushed, angry voices.

"But, Will, it's just not working!"

The man was well-spoken with the same smooth accent as Will. Georgia wondered if he was a member of Will's family, although he looked too young to be his father. Also, he was very blonde, unlike Will. The man continued, his voice growing louder. "You only just scraped the qualification, and everything's gone downhill since then. That mare's had her day, and so have you. We'll be a laughing stock if you go."

"Just give us another chance." Will's voice was low, pleading.

Georgia didn't know what to do – should she stay in her stable listening or make her escape and be seen? Deciding to stay put, she placed her arms around Lily's neck, still feeling guilty about how badly she had ridden her earlier. Lily snuffled against her, always forgiving, but swivelling her ears at the same time – obviously picking up on the tension in the yard. Georgia was just wondering

how long she was going to be stuck in Lily's stable
when she heard the sound of leather boots ringing
against the cobbled yard and realised that the man
must have stormed off in anger.

She hung back for another minute and then
quietly let herself out of Lily's stable, hoping to
hang the tack back up and grab her bike from
beside the yard gate. But, instead, Georgia
walked straight into Will, who had Santa's bridle
slung over his shoulder. He looked stressed and
distracted and Georgia felt incredibly awkward at
having overheard his conversation.

"Um, hi Will." She looked down and fiddled
with the cheek pieces of Lily's bridle.

"Georgia…" Will looked serious, pale and
drawn. "You won't tell Melanie about this, will
you?"

"About what?" Georgia was curious now. "Was
that not, um, your brother or something?" The

words died on her lips as she looked at Will, whose face had darkened.

"That's not my brother. It's because of my brother we're in this mess," he hissed, walking purposefully towards the tack room, followed by Georgia, who felt very confused.

"Look, forget it, OK?" Will waved her aside. "It's nothing to do with anyone but me and Ryan, OK?" He jerked his head in the direction of the fast-departing blue saloon and gave a wry smile. "Honestly, Georgia, if only all I had to worry was a few nerves." He sat down heavily on the old wooden bench in the yard. Suddenly he looked really pale and shaky.

"Will, are you OK?" Georgia asked anxiously. He didn't look well at all – his hair clung to his damp forehead and there were dark circles under his eyes.

"I'm fine. Just forget it," Will replied abruptly,

pulling himself up and barging out of the tack room in the direction of the house, leaving Georgia standing in the yard, trying to work out what had just happened.

Whatever it was, that man's visit had certainly shaken Will's confidence. Georgia sighed heavily. She wished she could help, but Will wasn't being very forthcoming. The one thing she was certain of was that she wasn't the only one at Redgrove covering up her true feelings.

✿ ✿ ✿

"Ready, Georgia?" Melanie had the keys to her 4×4 in one hand, and a stainless-steel flask of coffee in the other. It was the next day and, instead of riding, Georgia and Melanie were making their way to a large out-of-town saddlery that opened late for a couple of evenings a week. Melanie had asked Will if he would mind riding out with Santa while leading Lily, since the two mares seemed to

71

get on so well, so that she and Georgia had time to get their shopping done for the championships. Will had agreed, but Georgia was glad it had been Melanie who had asked. He had been very subdued since their conversation the previous night and he clearly had a lot on his mind.

Georgia adored visiting the tack shop; the enticing smell of new leather and saddle soap and all the gorgeous accessories she longed to buy for Lily – sparkly brow-bands, checked woollen rugs, brightly coloured bandages – the list was endless. She had a little pocket money saved up and she and Melanie were going to get some final bits for the Horse of the Year Show – some new gloves to replace Georgia's well-worn pair, and some travel accessories for Lily as she would be staying overnight at the championships in a temporary stable. Lily had never stayed away overnight before and Georgia hoped that she would be

OK. Melanie had assured her that horses didn't normally mind being away from home as long as their own handlers settled them in.

The shop was quiet, with only half an hour to go until closing time, but it gave Georgia and Melanie a chance to pick up all the items they needed. While waiting at the counter to pay, Melanie looked over a small display in a glass counter, and smiled. "Here, Georgia," she said, picking up a delicate silver tie pin with a sparkly silver horseshoe in the centre. "I think this would be the perfect thing to bring you luck. What do you think? My treat."

Georgia examined the pin, which was really beautiful. "No, please don't worry, Melanie," she said, feeling put on the spot.

"I insist!" Melanie chuckled, handing the pin over to the man behind the till. "It's not every day you get to ride at the Horse of the Year Show. Let's make it really special!"

As they left the shop with their small bag of items, Georgia clutched the little box containing the tie pin, her nerves rising once again. For the millionth time she wondered why she hadn't taken the opportunity to tell Melanie how nervous she was. Perhaps the little pin would bring her luck. The way her practice sessions were going, she was going to need it!

"You're quiet. Are you OK, Georgia?" Melanie asked, glancing at her as they drove home.

Georgia was still clutching the pin box in her hand, thinking about what the next few days would hold, and also thinking about Dan, and hoping things were OK between them. He was so easy-going and kind, which made her feel even worse about snapping at him. He had barely spoken to her at school, and had chosen to spend lunch with some of his friends from the rugby team.

"Sorry, Melanie. I'm just tired." Georgia tried to smile, but also stretched and yawned. She really was tired. She couldn't sleep very well and her dreams were often punctuated by disasters happening at the Horse of the Year Show, like falling off, Lily refusing to enter the ring, or worse. If only she had admitted to Dan how nervous she was, she would have been able to text him when she couldn't sleep, but she couldn't – not after the way she had spoken to him. That would be admitting the truth and Georgia had made up her mind that she wasn't going to let on to anyone about how she was really feeling.

Melanie looked concerned. "I think a rest for both you and Lily after the championships will do you good, G. You've been working really hard," she said. "We can turn her out for a month, let her have a breather, and bring her slowly back into work after Christmas. What do you think?"

Georgia nodded. That sounded great actually. She could just go up and groom her little mare, take her on walks. In fact, it sounded like heaven!

Melanie smiled, her eyes brightening as she continued cheerfully, "Isn't it exciting? Off to the Horse of the Year Show in a few days!"

The thought of *after* the Show had made Georgia feel a whole lot better, but Melanie's enthusiasm for the big day brought her crashing back down to the ground with a bump.

The 4×4 wended its way towards home. As they turned off the main road a couple of miles from Redgrove, Melanie suddenly pointed to a small house that lay back from the junction. Georgia didn't go on this route much, as it wasn't on the way to school, or the way the bus into town went, so she only vaguely recognised where she was.

"That's where Will and his brother used to live." Melanie gestured towards the house. "A few years ago now. I can't believe they still haven't sold the place. Mind you, it's a bit overgrown."

It was a pretty, if slightly worn-looking cottage with a small paddock adjoining it and some tumbledown farm buildings situated further back. A "For Sale" sign stood in the garden, but the house looked completely deserted.

"Oh?" Georgia's interest was roused. "Why did they move?" She thought the cottage looked really sweet, and had always longed for a paddock right next to her house. But it looked a million miles away from Will's current world, with his brother's fancy yard, horse walker and sponsored horsebox.

"Well, it was a while ago now," Melanie explained. "Jasper's a lot older than you and Will, remember. Jasper was the star member of the Round Barrow Pony Club. He was Janey's favourite, but then he got noticed by this sponsor and they moved, and he set up in his own yard, from what I gather. I guess Will just followed in his footsteps as well. He always hero-worshipped Jasper. His mum – I was never sure where his father lived – moved to London when they got their deal – something to do with her work. She was never horsey. It was all driven by Jasper." Melanie slowed the car right down, allowing Georgia to gaze up a bumpy drive towards the cottage. "Jasper is Will's guardian, but it can't be easy for Will, having such a well-known older brother to live up to. He was always so good with the young ponies, I remember," Melanie mused out loud.

From what Georgia knew of Will, she couldn't imagine him and Santa living here; it was so different from their big flashy yard, which he had shown her countless photos of on his mobile phone.

Georgia realised that it would be a dream come true to live in a little cottage with her mum, with Lily in a paddock next door! Smiling sadly to herself, she thought that maybe she wasn't cut out to be a big show rider with her own yard, after all!

Chapter Eight

"So, tell me what he said again." Emma was sitting cross-legged on her bed on Friday evening, painting her toenails, eating pizza and listening to Georgia's account of the week's events. With all the build-up to the Horse of the Year Show, Georgia realised that she and Emma had barely had a chance to hang out together for a while. Her mum had encouraged her to go round for the evening, telling her to forget about the Show for a few hours.

Georgia knew her mum was right. She had neglected her friends a bit lately. Things were still strained with Dan, although Georgia had apologised for her snappiness at least twice. Being Dan, he had just waved it off with his usual easy-going style, but Georgia could tell he was hurt, and there was a real distance between them. Remembering Melanie's suggestion to give Lily a break following the championships, Georgia decided she would be glad when the Show was over and she could concentrate on just enjoying her little palomino pony, and also hanging out with her friends!

"I've told you, Em." Georgia paused between mouthfuls, thinking again about her recent strange encounter with Will and the man watching him jump. "It wasn't his brother, or any relation to him, I don't think. Will said his name was Ryan. But whoever he was, he didn't seem at all happy with Will!"

"Hmm. I wonder what's going on..." Emma loved mysteries and yard gossip. Pulling her laptop out from under the bed, she pressed the start button and tapped away for a few seconds, gazing at the screen.

"What are you doing, Em?" Georgia reached across her friend for a slice of pizza.

Emma turned the computer round and showed Georgia the screen. "Digging," she said in a mysterious tone.

Georgia, who didn't spend much time on the Internet, gazed at the screen. There was a picture of the most beautiful dark-brown mare jumping over a rustic-looking gate. She looked familiar. Squinting, Georgia realised why. It was Santa! But that wasn't Will riding her, she was sure about that. It looked like him – the same dark hair and arrogant expression – but this man was much older, probably in his mid-twenties.

"Look here." Emma turned the laptop back round and started reading the paragraph underneath the photo. "Jasper Bowen. Isn't 'Bowen' Will's surname?"

Georgia nodded, remembering her conversation with Will when he had asked her if she had heard of his brother.

Emma looked at the picture again. "He *is* good-looking, you know – a bit like Will."

"Emma!" Georgia giggled "I *knew* you liked Will!"

Blushing and grinning, Emma carried on reading, but it wasn't long before she frowned, and her laughter subsided.

"What's up, Em?" Georgia asked, curious at her best friend's sudden change in tone.

"I don't know. It looks like Will's brother is in trouble. I can't really work it out. Here, Georgia, you read."

Passing over the laptop, she resumed her cross-legged position as Georgia slowly read the page, her finger following each sentence. It was some sort of horsey gossip column, and there were a lot of pictures of Jasper and Santa, plus a few other gorgeous-looking ponies, all jumping. Georgia was used to the smart world of flat native showing, which tended to be more tweed and ribbons. This was altogether flashier. The ponies' manes were all neatly plaited and their tack was polished to a high shine. Jasper was wearing a very expensive-looking jacket.

"'Darling of the working hunter jumping world falls out with sponsor'," she read out loud. "'Following his terrible accident in May, Jasper Bowen, former National Working Hunter

Champion, has fallen out with the most enviable sponsor in showing – Ryan Cartwright of Diamond Horses. Who's going to back Jasper's yard and ponies now?'" The words screamed out to Georgia with all the brashness of a tabloid paper. "'It falls to Jasper's younger brother, William Bowen, to carry on the family name at this year's Horse of the Year Show with the Bowens' schoolmistress, nineteen-year-old Santa, or the Bowens may lose everything, including their ponies!'"

Feeling a bit sick, Georgia closed the page. She couldn't read any more. The man who was in the yard the other day must have been Ryan Cartwright. And Santa was a much older pony than she had thought, although Georgia would have never have guessed she was nineteen – a schoolmistress – and obviously well known, judging by the amount of web entries there were dedicated to her and Jasper. She had won countless rosettes and championships over the years. No wonder Will was so proud of her. But was she capable of jumping the same big tracks as before, Georgia wondered, remembering the mare's refusals? She knew the jumps at the championships were always higher than at the qualifying shows. And what had Jasper done to fall out with his sponsor? And why was it up to Will to make things better? There were so many unanswered questions.

Putting her slice of pizza down, Georgia suddenly didn't feel hungry any more. Will was right – all she had to worry about were a few nerves. She remembered the little cottage with the paddock that Melanie had pointed out to her the other day. It seemed a world away from Will's life now. Will was riding to win – and with so much counting on it.

Lily's creamy mane flew up and down in time with her strides, barely making a sound as she moved through the long grass of the bottom meadow. It was going to be one of those glorious autumn days when you could still almost pretend it was summer, were it not for the abundance of blackberries in the hedges and the yellowing of the leaves around the yard. Georgia breathed in and out in time with Lily's canter strides as she powered up the long side of the meadow where Simon had cut a path with his mini tractor.

It was a perfect, still morning, long before breakfast, and certainly earlier than most non-horsey people rose on a Sunday. It was also Georgia's favourite time of the day. Everything about it was so far removed from the razzle-dazzle of the show ring and if Georgia just concentrated on her cantering, she could pretend she didn't have to take part soon in the biggest Show of her life. Georgia always rode beautifully when she was just out hacking, with no one watching. Following her disastrous lesson with Janey a few nights ago, she had managed to bluff it out with Melanie, reassuring her that it had just been an off day. Melanie was so full of her own excitement over Sophie's planned trip home for the championships that she had not needed much convincing. After all, Georgia had been so excited to qualify all those months ago, there was no reason to think otherwise.

Georgia felt awful about lying to her. She had managed a better lesson the previous night with Melanie, although it was still nowhere near her normal standard of relaxed riding. Her Friday evening discovery at Emma's house was still playing on her mind. She hadn't seen Will all weekend – he must have ridden later than her, or just been at the yard when she wasn't there. She

probably wouldn't see him today either because later that day she was going to go and help Dan at the farm for a while. It had been arranged ages ago, before their misunderstanding, and Georgia knew she needed to try and make it up to him. She had sent him a couple of texts, both of which had gone unanswered.

Untacking Lily back at the yard, Georgia gazed at the sky and wondered what to do. Despite the chilly start to the morning, it was going to be warm, and she didn't want to rug her little mare up to turn her out. Instead, she decided to turn her out just as she was so that Lily could get the chance to enjoy a roll, and have the autumn sun on her back for a few hours.

After hacking out Wilson, giving Callie a good groom, and making sure all the stables were ready for the evening, Georgia picked up her bike and set off for Dan's farm. Her tummy was grumbling –

it was definitely time for breakfast now, and luckily Dan must have been thinking the same because there was an enticing smell of frying bacon drifting out of the farmhouse window.

"Morning, Georgia." Dan's older brother Ben let her into the house, grinning as always.

"Morning, Ben," Georgia replied, blushing slightly. He would no doubt be teasing Dan later, convinced that he and Georgia were an item!

"Hey, G." Dan's face was slightly flushed from cooking the breakfast. Passing Georgia a bacon sandwich wrapped in a piece of kitchen towel, he started to pull on his boots beside the back door, without making further conversation. Ben, noticing the awkwardness between the two of them, raised an eyebrow, but to Georgia's relief he decided not to say anything. She followed Dan out of the back door in silence, glad he hadn't told her to go away.

For the rest of the morning, Georgia threw herself into her work, grateful for the distraction. She wasn't afraid of getting her hands dirty and happily helped feed the calves and fork fresh straw into their pens. It meant Dan's dad was free to serve in the farm shop, which was always busy on a Sunday with customers looking to buy the meat for their lunch or eggs for a late breakfast. Georgia was glad the shop was doing well. They had come so close to losing it all after a property developer tried to force them off their land a year earlier. It was brilliant to see how quickly the farm and family had turned itself around!

As Georgia and Dan worked, they chatted about school, their classmates and even their dogs – anything really to avoid talking about the Horse of the Year Show. It seemed to Georgia that Dan was deliberately avoiding the subject of horses. However, she couldn't help but tell Dan her worries about Will, and what she and Emma had found out on Friday evening.

Dan looked genuinely puzzled when she finished, and, like Georgia, asked the most obvious question. "Why would the family be in trouble?" he said. "Perhaps it's just gossip. Do you really think you should believe everything you read?" The way he said it was a bit harsh, but Georgia knew he didn't mean it unkindly – he just knew Georgia's tendency to walk into drama, and her concern for every pony she ever met!

"I don't know." Georgia chewed on her thumbnail. "But I do know that something is wrong!"

"But Melanie said she would keep an eye on Will, didn't she?" Dan still looked confused.

"Yes." Georgia shrugged. "I guess she did, and I'm sure she will. Just as long as Santa's OK – that's

what I'm worried about."

"And what about you?" Dan said, changing the subject, but Georgia knew what he meant. He could see straight through her, even if she had managed to convince Melanie, Mum and Emma that she was fine and not suffering from nerves. "What about that lesson the other day?"

"Don't, Dan!" Georgia said angrily. "I told you that was an off day. Why won't you believe me?"

Dan just raised an eyebrow and carried on fluffing up the calves' straw beds.

Georgia groaned inwardly. Having spent the morning together, she'd hoped that things would be OK between her and Dan, but now they were back to square one. She knew that *he* knew she was covering up her true feelings and she could tell that he was annoyed with her for not being more open with him. Again, she wondered why she was putting herself through all of this. But her course was set now and it was too late to pull out.

Perhaps the best thing was to stay out of Dan's way – just until the Show was over.

CHAPTER NINE

The sun had gone in by the time Georgia had finished helping Dan. There was a chill to the breeze, and a few drops of rain had started to fall. Georgia knew Dan probably needed more help, but he'd said she could head off just before he went in for his lunch. Things definitely weren't right between them, Georgia thought with a sigh. Remembering Lily was out without a rug on, Georgia climbed on her bike and started to cycle back to Redgrove. Although Lily was a Welsh mountain pony, her Horse of the Year Show preparation included hours of extra grooming, and as a result her coat was fine and silky. So she was also a pony who felt the cold!

Opening the yard gates, Georgia was surprised to see the dark-blue saloon from the other evening back again. There was no sign of Melanie's car, though, and the yard was quiet. Hurrying to the tack room, Georgia grabbed Lily and Wilson's medium-weight turnouts and carried them over to the paddock, where she quickly rugged up the two ponies. Lily seemed a little on edge and kept gazing towards the outdoor school, where her new friend Santa was being ridden.

There was a definite atmosphere in the school. Ryan was leaning against the arena fence, watching Will jump a course. The jumps were lower than the grid Will had been jumping during the previous week and Santa looked a lot happier. Her eager face lit up as she soared the lower course, which was no higher than the jumps Georgia might have attempted in the past with Wilson.

"I told you..." Will's voice carried over to Georgia on the breeze. "She is capable, just give us one last chance."

Neither he nor Ryan seemed to have noticed she was there, or maybe they just didn't care that she was watching. Ryan straightened up, looking angry. He appeared to be arguing with Will, but Georgia couldn't make out the words. His stance was menacing though, and she looked around, suddenly feeling a little afraid.

Then, to Georgia's relief, Melanie strode through the yard gates and, immediately taking stock of the situation, she marched up to Ryan. "I know who you are and I'd like you to get off my property," she said firmly.

Ryan laughed, continuing to lean against the fence. "You can't, I'm the sponsor of this pony. I *own* her." He glanced at Will before adding in a malicious voice, "For now." Then, aggressively, he swung back to face Melanie.

"I couldn't care less if you own her." Melanie was not easily scared and stood her ground. "Either you leave, right now, or I call the police."

Ryan hesitated for a moment. Then, gathering up his coat, he turned and stalked back to his car, but not before delivering a parting shot. "Riders like you are two a penny, Will Bowen. Don't you forget it!"

☆ ☆ ☆

As soon as Ryan's car had sped down the drive, Melanie turned to Will, who had shakily dismounted from Santa and was starting to lead her back towards her stable. "Not so fast, young man," she said firmly. "I think you have some explaining to do." Melanie glanced at Georgia, who was still in the field with the ponies, and beckoned her over. "Georgia, you come as well. We're going to sort this out – I won't have secrets in my yard."

Once Santa was untacked, rugged and back out in her paddock, Georgia, Will and Melanie sat down in the tack room. Georgia noticed that Will's hands were trembling slightly. Feeling a little awkward, Georgia twisted a lead rope round and round in her fingers.

"So, Will." Melanie's voice was still firm, but kinder now. "Can you tell me what's going on?"

"Honestly, it's nothing," Will mumbled, his eyes firmly fixed on a piece of straw on the ground.

"Well, it didn't look like nothing," Melanie said. "And if you aren't going to tell me, then I'm afraid I'll have no choice but to send you *and* Santa back home. I can't have people like that man coming in and out of my yard. You do understand, don't you?"

Will nodded, his eyes still down. "Please, please let me stay." His voice was so quiet, Georgia could barely hear him.

Trembling, he explained that Ryan Cartwright, the owner of Diamond Horses, had been happy to sponsor his brother Jasper while he won championship after championship, becoming one of the best-known show riders around. But that had all changed when Jasper had taken a bad fall at the beginning of the season and hadn't fully regained his confidence. Every time Jasper competed, he would invariably end up eliminated, or placed down the line. His talent lay with working with the younger horses on the ground, and it had been up to Will to carry on competing the ponies in his brother's place. But the pressure had been getting too much, and Ryan was tiring of sponsoring a yard that wasn't producing the same results it once did.

"I've had too many last chances," Will said, looking down at his hands. He sounded close to tears. "I'll never be as good as Jasper, and I've let him down."

Melanie looked perplexed. "Do you need the sponsorship?" she said in a confused voice. "Surely Jasper must have something of his own after all those years of riding?"

Will shook his head, reddening slightly. "Everything is owned by Ryan – the ponies, the lorry, the yard. Everyone thinks we must be loaded but we don't have a penny to our name. Jasper never planned ahead. He wasn't that much older than I am now when he got the sponsorship deal, and he thought it would last forever. I love all of the horses, especially the youngsters, but Santa's special. If we lose the Diamond Horses' deal, then she'll be sold, and we won't be able to afford to buy her."

He looked up, his face anguished. "Even with her track record, she won't fetch much at her age, so she'll be sold to someone who doesn't understand her. They'll just make her jump and jump until she breaks down, and then she'll end up in market, and then..." He let out a little sob. "We've had her for over ten years. She can't go."

"Is that why you came back here?" Melanie asked gently.

Will nodded, gazing at the wall as he spoke. "Jasper's buried his head in the sand, not admitting that we're going to lose the yard. He's looking at bank loans and everything, but I thought if I just had one good ride at the Horse of the Year Show – Santa's last championship – then Ryan might not end the sponsorship. Jasper didn't want me to try, but he couldn't stop me. I used the last bit of my savings to hire a trailer and pay Janey for my lessons, but it's no good, it's not going to work out." Will put his head in his hands and muttered, "Ryan doesn't think I'm good enough, and Santa's lost her nerve. Oh, I'm sorry, Melanie. I shouldn't have got you involved in this mess."

"Don't apologise to me," Melanie said kindly. "You poor thing, with all that pressure on your shoulders. I'll tell you what I'm going to do. I'm going to ring up Sara and get her to send your brother down here. He's the one that needs to sort this out, not you." Then, gently, she continued. "Will, you *are* a talented rider – easily as talented as your brother – but you're too young to take all of this on. Ryan can't just back out of a sponsorship deal – there has to be some sort of contract. Everything can always be sorted out," she said reassuringly.

"As easy as that?" Will said, looking dubious, but sounding hopeful.

Georgia knew from past experience that problems were always better if you shared them with someone, especially a grown-up like Melanie.

Dusting her hands off, Melanie stood up. "Will, don't worry any more. I'll make some phone calls, and get your brother down here. Maybe Janey can have a word with him as well." Then, smiling broadly, she continued, "Tell you what – Simon was going to get fish and chips tonight. What do you say to a yard supper? Invite Emma and Dan over if you want to, Georgia. And call your mum as well, so she knows where you are."

Will and Georgia looked at each other and smiled, and then both nodded in unison. That sounded like a great idea!

"Now, go and finish off the ponies." Melanie nodded in the direction of the loose boxes.

Georgia and Will hurried off and finished up the yard chores together. Now that the pressure was off him a little, Will chatted away and Georgia was surprised to find that he was actually a really nice person. All his arrogance and bravado were clearly part of an act. They had quite a lot in common too – it turned out that Will knew Josephine Smalley well and they chatted easily about the riders from her yard and the gorgeous ponies.

At last Emma joined them, blushing and giggling every time Will spoke to her. "Where's Dan?" she asked curiously as Georgia checked her phone again.

Georgia sighed. He obviously wasn't coming. *And who could blame him*, she thought sadly. It was her own fault. Emma raised an eyebrow, but didn't say anything.

The four ponies watched the proceedings with interest – Santa glued to her new friend Lily's side. Later, sitting on rugs in the tack room and tucking into the delicious fish and chips, Georgia felt slightly better – about the ponies anyway. And, considering all that Will had been going through, surely she could face riding in the championships, given there was no real pressure on her at all? She sighed. She just wished that she and Dan were OK. Still, there would be plenty of time after the Show to get everything back on track.

Pleased with her more positive frame of mind, Georgia kissed Lily goodnight. Then Melanie dropped both her and Emma back home.

That night, for the first time in ages, Georgia slept really well. With only a couple of days left until the horsebox left for the Horse of the Year Show, she certainly needed it. And waking up the next morning feeling less tired made her feel more positive about her prospects at the Show. Maybe, just maybe, she'd been worrying for no reason, and everything would work out just fine!

CHAPTER TEN

Georgia got the text after school the next afternoon. She was waiting at the bus stop with Emma, her school bag held over her head as she tried to keep dry. Dan was nearby with one of his rugby friends. They had been perfectly polite to each other at school, but Dan had just nodded when Georgia had told him she was feeling better about everything and was definitely going to ride at the championships. She heard a familiar beep from her pocket and, retrieving the phone, she squinted at the screen. She had to read the message a couple of times for it to sink in. The message was from Melanie, and it was serious.

Have you heard from Will?? He and Santa have disappeared.

☆ ☆ ☆

The bus ride home seemed to take forever. Dropping Dan and Emma off first, who promised they would come up to the yard later if needed, the bus continued through the winding village lanes until it stopped just outside Georgia's cottage. Jumping out, Georgia tore down the overgrown path, ready to change into her yard clothes.

Her mum was in the kitchen, stirring something on the hob with Pip lying at her feet. She smiled when she saw her daughter. "Hi, sweetheart!" she said as Georgia bounded up the stairs two at a time.

"Hi, Mum," Georgia called, reappearing a minute later in her old jeans and sweater. "I'm off to the yard!"

"Oh." Her mum looked slightly crestfallen. "I thought you gave Lily Mondays off and that we could spend some time together. I've made you your favourite, spaghetti bolognaise. I thought we could eat it in front of the television and have a relaxed evening. You've been so busy lately…" Her voice trailed off.

Georgia, feeling guilty, kissed her mum on the cheek. "Sorry, Mum, I really am – but there's an emergency at the yard. I'll tell you about it later."

"All right then," her mum said, continuing to stir. "But, Georgia, make sure you're not letting your schoolwork slip. You remember what happened last time?" Her words barely reached Georgia, who was already out of the door and grabbing her bike.

☆ ☆ ☆

When Georgia shot through the yard gates, she discovered that Redgrove was buzzing with activity. A police car was parked next to the horse lorry and there was a policeman deep in conversation with Melanie, who looked pale with worry. On seeing Georgia, she quickly beckoned her over. The policeman was a kindly-looking man but, even so, Georgia felt herself gulp. She had never really had to deal with the police before, apart from when Lily's previous owner had tried to steal her back.

"When did you last see the young man in question?" the policeman asked. He had a gruff, but not unkind voice.

"Um, last night," Georgia stammered. "We all

had fish and chips here, with Melanie, and my friend, Emma." She turned to Melanie, confused. "What's going on?"

Excusing herself from the policeman, who was taking notes, Melanie told Georgia that after making a few phone calls in the morning, including one to Will's aunt, she had been able to tell him that the situation with his sponsor could be sorted out and Ryan would back off. Will had seemed happy enough, she said, and had asked if he could stay for a couple more days with Santa, and perhaps help Georgia with her show prep. The last Melanie had seen of him was after breakfast when she left to go into town to run some errands. Will had been happily tacking up Santa, ready to go for a hack over the heath. When she came home, he wasn't back, but she hadn't thought any more about it until the afternoon when she noticed Lily pacing up and down the fence line of her field, searching for her friend. Melanie had quickly worked out that over seven hours had passed since Will had left.

"What if he fell while he was out on the ride? Or Santa has had an accident?" Georgia's blood ran cold at the thought of the pretty brown pony lying somewhere on the heath, or, worse still, having been hit by a car on the road.

Melanie shook her head, pale now. "That was my first thought as well, G," she said anxiously, running a hand through her dark hair. "But I don't think so." Briefly, she explained to Georgia that after realising Will hadn't returned, she had gone to the tack room to find Santa's head collar, and found it wasn't there. Nor was Santa's cotton day-sheet. Running up to Will's room, she'd found most of his belongings still there, including his shiny black boots and tweed jacket, waiting for the Horse of the Year Show, but there was a small rucksack missing and a few essential items. It looked as if he'd thought carefully about what he and Santa would need, before he'd set off. Prior to phoning the police, Melanie had called his brother, his mum and Sara. None of them knew where Will and Santa were.

"It seems he's disappeared deliberately," Melanie said, sounding shaky.

Simon, who had also been talking to the policeman, placed a hand over her arm. "It's not your fault," he said in a soothing voice.

"It feels like it!" Melanie wailed. "I reassured him yesterday that we could sort out this mess but he obviously didn't think it was really going to happen … and now he and Santa could be anywhere. It's *all* my fault. I know he acts older, but he's only a child, really. What if something happens to him?" Sitting on the mounting block, Melanie pulled out her phone. "I've texted and rung him, but there's no answer."

She tried ringing again but the call went straight to Will's answer phone. "See!" Melanie sounded desperate now, showing Georgia, the phone. "Georgia, maybe you could try him a few times?"

Georgia nodded, and promised she would. She felt awful as well. Firstly for being so judgemental about Will when he arrived, not realising what he had been dealing with, and secondly for making such a big deal about her worries over the Horse of the Year Show when Will faced far bigger issues. At least Lily would always be safe. Who knew what the future held for Santa now...

☆ ☆ ☆

Just then, a huge cream and black lorry purred into the yard. Jumping up, frowning, Georgia shielded her eyes against the late afternoon sun, trying to work out who it was.

A woman hopped out of the cab, smartly

114

dressed in checked breeches. A winged Pegasus and the words *Flying Horses Transport* were emblazoned on the back of her jacket. She looked as though she meant business. Flicking through a notebook in her hand she turned to Melanie. "Is this Redgrove Farm?"

"Yes, it is," Melanie said, sounding a little cool.

Undeterred, the woman carried on. "We're picking up a pony for a Mr Ryan Cartwright from this address. Is she ready?"

Melanie looked appalled. "Ready?" she said in a horrified voice. "You mean Ryan has sold Santa?"

The woman threw her hands up. "Look, I don't know," she said, clearly exasperated. "We were booked to pick up a mare and drop her at a new address, that's all I was told. I don't care much for the ins and outs."

Narrowing her eyes, Melanie looked at the woman. "Can you at least tell me where the pony is meant to be going?"

The woman consulted her phone. "Some fancy dealers," she said, clearly not wanting to give too much away.

Georgia heard Melanie draw in her breath. She couldn't believe Santa was being sold, just like that.

"You can't take the mare," Melanie said firmly. "Not least because nobody knows where she is!"

The woman scowled. "So you mean to tell me that I've come all this way for nothing?"

"Yes, I'm afraid it would seem so," Melanie replied, gesturing towards the policeman still waiting in the yard. "Now, if you don't mind, I've got more important things to deal with."

Once the woman had climbed back in her cab, muttering angrily under her breath, and the huge lorry had manoeuvred its way back out of the yard gates, Melanie turned to Georgia. "I've had an idea," she said. "If we can just get hold of Will, and I can explain my plan to him, then maybe he will feel reassured enough to come back to Redgrove. Do you mind finishing off the evening stables? I've got to go inside and make some calls."

Still feeling shaken, but pleased to occupy herself, Georgia set to work. Despite the drama, Wilson, Callie and Lily still needed attending to – their straw beds had to be laid for the night and their feeds making up. She wondered what Melanie had up her sleeve. Whatever it was, she hoped it would mean Will could somehow keep Santa. But more than that, she hoped that Will, and his beautiful kind mare, were safe.

CHAPTER ELEVEN

The night passed with no sign of Will or his pony. After going home, leaving Melanie sitting at the kitchen table, Georgia kept her phone right next to her bed just in case Melanie texted her, as she had promised to do if there was any news. But, despite waking up at least five times in the night and checking her phone, there was no message. Eventually, early next morning, and unable to sleep, Georgia sat with her mum and Pip in the kitchen, nursing a cup of tea and waiting until she could head over to the stables.

It was the day they should have been leaving for the Horse of the Year Show, but it was almost certain that the dark-green horse lorry wouldn't be going now. Georgia had been so busy worrying about Will and Santa that, for the first time in ages, she hadn't given the Show a second thought. It was only because her mum mentioned it to her as she left the house that it was at the forefront of her mind now. Yet it seemed so trivial compared to what Will must be going through now.

The atmosphere was sombre at the yard as Georgia pushed her bike through the gates. There was still no familiar dark-brown head in the stable next to Lily's. Georgia had started to pack up the lorry in preparation a couple of days before, but as the day wore on and there was still no sign of

Will, it looked likely that they would all be staying at Redgrove.

"There will always be next year…" a bitterly disappointed Melanie had reassured Georgia. Not wanting to throw away Georgia's big chance, she had talked about them going anyway and Simon holding the fort, but both of them knew that their hearts wouldn't be in it and that it would feel wrong to compete with Will missing.

Georgia couldn't help but feel guilty – after all, she had wished so many times that she wasn't going, and now it looked as though that was going to come true. She ran a hand over the soft brown leather of her show bridle, which hung clean, oiled and sparkling in the tack room, and swallowed hard. She knew the most important thing now was to find Will and Santa and make sure they were safe, but even so, a tiny part of her couldn't help but feel sorry for herself. There would always be other years, she knew that. But now that she was so nearly there, she was scared she would never want to try again, knowing how much the build-up to the Show had terrified her this time round.

"Tell you what, Georgia," Melanie said, sounding exhausted as they led Callie, Wilson and Lily back in from the fields that afternoon. "Why don't you take Lily out for a nice ride this evening, before it gets dark? There's not much more that can be done here."

"Really?" said Georgia.

"Yes, really. You need some time-out," said Melanie firmly. "A good canter always clears away the cobwebs. Enjoy yourself. I'll phone you straight away if there's any news. And, Georgia…" Hesitating, Melanie suddenly looked really sad. "I'm so sorry we can't go to the championships. Thanks for being so understanding."

Nodding sadly, Georgia set off to get Lily. Really, the championships didn't matter, in comparison with what was happening here. Carefully, she took her tack down from its position in the tack room and, looping the bridle over her shoulder, walked down to Lily's stable, where the palomino was standing, stock-still, occasionally thrusting her head forwards, her amber eyes catching the light. She did seem a little on edge.

"Easy, my beauty…" Crooning to her, Georgia quickly tacked up the little mare. She was so clean from the rigorous grooming and bathing routine Georgia had been giving her that she only needed a quick dust off.

In no time at all, Georgia was ready, scarf pulled up over her nose, clattering over the cobbles and out through the gates on to the heathland beyond the yard. It was a glorious late afternoon, and the trees bordering the neat cobbled yard were starting to change to deep reds and golds. It was still quite cold, though, and Georgia was grateful to her mum for making her dress up warmly before she had left that morning.

Lily shied uncharacteristically at a sign on the small lane, snorting and plunging.

"Hey, girl…" Georgia gently scratched the little mare on her withers, calming her down. It was probably due to the fact that Georgia hadn't ridden her for a couple of days and she was super-fit and fresh. The cold weather could make ponies a little skittish.

Once they were out on the heath, Georgia let Lily have her head. It felt amazing, Lily's strong legs eating up the ground and her champagne-coloured tail streaming behind her. It was a real shame, Georgia reflected, that the judges wouldn't see her in the ring, looking her best. Now she was unable to go, it seemed so silly that she'd got in such a state about it. She should have just enjoyed the build up to the Show instead!

Continuing up the long ridgeway that sat above the pretty village of Redgrove, Lily was still pulling forwards, fresh and eager. The valley below them, one side sloping away towards Dan's farm, and the other down towards the neighbouring villages, looked magical in the cold, late afternoon light, with the houses and cars like little toy models.

"Come on, Lily." Eager to get her pony back to her warm stable and rugs, and to get a hot drink for herself, Georgia gently guided the little palomino back towards home, softly shifting her weight in the saddle and easing her right rein towards the track that led back to Redgrove.

Expecting Lily to quietly head towards home, she relaxed in the saddle, letting her reins slacken, but the palomino stopped suddenly and threw her head towards Georgia, catching her smartly on the nose and instantly causing it to bleed.

"Ouch, Lily!" Georgia cried. Her nose started to sting, and she felt a warmth trickle down her chin. Holding the reins in one hand, she wiped away the blood with the back of her gloved free hand, and tried to ignore the pain. But she was worried – Lily never behaved like this. Remembering how Jemma had frightened the little palomino by forcing her to go forwards with a whip when she had been reluctant and scared, Georgia did her best to remain quiet and calm.

"Come on, girl," she said as gently as possible, again trying to guide the little mare back towards the stables.

It was starting to get dusky now; the evening sky was awash with pink and grey clouds. Again, Lily planted, backing up so suddenly that Georgia was nearly unseated. It was no good; Lily didn't want to go forwards at all. She tossed her head, snorting, the sound carrying across the quiet valley.

"Would you rather I led you?" Patting her, Georgia slipped out of the saddle and placed a reassuring hand on Lily's neck, drawing the reins over her head, trying to soothe her. It was very rare that she needed to get off and lead Lily, but something had obviously worried the little mare and, with the evening drawing in, Georgia wanted to get her home as quickly as possible. "Come on, sweetheart."

Clicking her tongue, Georgia started to lead Lily forwards towards the gate that took them off the hill and on to the path towards home.

Reluctantly, Lily followed her. Stopping at the gate, Georgia struggled for a minute with the heavy, fiddly clasp, placing the reins back over the mare's head and into one hand as she did so. And that was all it took. Lily suddenly pulled back and in that moment she was free from Georgia's hold.

CHAPTER TWELVE

"Lily!" cried Georgia. Time seemed to stand still. She made a grab for the reins, just as Lily tossed her head into the air and trotted a few steps away.

Alarmed, Georgia pleaded with her little mare, willing her to stand quietly. It would be a total disaster if she was loose on the heath, which led to a main road at the bottom of the valley. Thinking fast, Georgia stepped forwards quietly, rustling a sweet paper in her pocket to try and get the palomino's attention. But it was no good. Lily hesitated, before spinning round and cantering a few paces away from Georgia, who was feeling increasingly panicked. Thank goodness she had put the reins back over her head, so Lily couldn't trip on them, but even so, anything could happen, and the worst *would* happen if she got on to the busy road.

Lily slowed a bit but was still steadily moving away from Georgia, towards the bottom of the valley and the main road. Crossing her fingers, Georgia prayed that the gate on to the bridleway was shut. Maybe Lily would stop there if it was, or maybe she would try and jump. She gave a small sob of fear as she hurried behind Lily, trying not to startle the little mare, whose head was as high as she could carry it and who was trotting like a hackney pony, her knees striking the air.

Taking care not to break into a run behind the palomino and frighten her even more, Georgia followed as quietly as she could, still rustling the sweet wrapper. Lily didn't gallop off, as she could have done, but equally she stayed a little way ahead of Georgia the whole time. They continued like this for a few long minutes.

Starting to cry, Georgia tripped and stumbled a couple of times as Lily descended down the chalk path, further and further from Redgrove. "Please, Lily!" she wailed, wishing they were back at the yard, Lily safely tucked up in her stable. There was just no way she could catch up with her pony, and the road was only a few hundred metres ahead. Lily was trotting at a steadier pace now. Exhausted, Georgia slowed. She was panting hard, her breath hanging in the cold, crisp air. She had to keep going.

She had a flashback to the day that she and Dan had followed Lily over the Welsh mountainside, when they had attempted to rescue her from Jemma, her former owner. But that was different; Lily had been running in a blind panic, full of fear. She seemed much calmer this time, never going too far from Georgia. It was totally out of character. It was almost as though she knew where she was heading.

Rounding the final bend, Georgia's heart was in her mouth as she heard cars and lorries whizzing by on the road. Although it was a country road, it was one of the main routes towards Redgrove and the surrounding villages, and it could get very busy. She cried with relief when she saw that the big wooden gates leading on to the bridleway were firmly closed, and even better, that Lily had come to a trembling halt in front of them.

"Lily!" Georgia's breath was coming out in great

heaving rasps now, tears streaking her face as she stumbled towards her pony, her legs buckling beneath her. Despite the chill, she was boiling hot under her jacket, but shivering with shock. Quickly getting hold of the little palomino's reins, she leaned her head against Lily's neck and cried for a few seconds into her creamy mane, feeling sick. She would never have forgiven herself if anything had happened to her beloved pony.

Lily blew into her hair before raising her head again and gazing into the distance. Every hair on her body seemed to twitch as she waved her delicate head from side to side, snorting.

"Lily, my darling…" Whispering gently to her, Georgia decided it would be safest to get back on, rather than risk losing the pony again if she plunged away. Swinging herself back into the saddle, her legs still trembling violently, she was just about to nudge the little mare back up the hill, when all of a sudden Lily quivered and let out a shrill high- pitched whinny, her nostrils flaring. And there, in return came a shrill answer, almost like an echo. Dancing from side to side, Lily repeated her call and, again, the same urgent cry came back. It was another pony, and it didn't sound far away!

☆ ☆ ☆

Trying to get her bearings, Georgia looked around her. She knew that Redgrove lay on the other side of the hill, and that she wasn't far away by road. It looked familiar. Suddenly she realised: she had been here before, on the way back from the saddler's – the day Melanie had bought her the lucky silver tie pin. The cottage, beyond the road on the opposite side, was Will's old house! And what's more, the shrill whinny was coming directly from the property.

Thinking fast, Georgia checked her jacket pocket

for her mobile phone. Thankfully, she hadn't left it in the tack room. Nudging Lily forwards, she leaned down and opened the gate that led them on to the bridleway, and on to the verge. Steadying the little palomino, Georgia waited, her heart in her mouth, for a clear moment to cross the road.

A car zipped by them at speed, followed by a van. Lily backed up nervously. Eventually the road was clear and Georgia urged Lily on at a trot, crossing over and reaching the long drive, just as another car flew past.

"Good girl, good brave girl." Georgia praised Lily as much as she could, knowing that the little mare was still nervous about roads. Yet now it was Lily who was eager to continue, her stride lengthening as they walked purposefully down the drive towards the cottage, and towards the shrill whinny that sounded much clearer now.

The house was still deserted, as it had been the

day Georgia had passed it with Melanie. Straining her ears, she realised the whinny was coming from the outbuildings, which lay further back. Dismounting and leading Lily forwards, Georgia called out.

"Hello?" Her voice echoed around the old stone buildings, bouncing off the cobbles. Then she heard it, loud and clear – horse's hooves against concrete. A pony was moving around in one of the buildings, and from the way the hooves were clattering, the pony was agitated! "Hello?" Georgia repeated, but again, there was no answer.

Looping Lily's reins over her arm, Georgia tried the door into the barn, where the whinnying was coming from. It was old and heavy, and seemed to be fastened from the inside. Peeking through the crack, Georgia gasped when she caught sight of a familiar dark-brown pony in one of the stalls at the far end. It was Santa!

CHAPTER THIRTEEN

But if Santa was here, where was Will?

Georgia pulled at the door again, widening the gap so she could peer into the barn. Old hay bales were stacked up next to the stall, plus a few bits of rusty machinery. Looking closer, Georgia saw a flash of bright blue under the hay. It looked like it was some sort of material, but what? Then she recognised it as Will's logo jacket – the one he had been wearing the day he had ridden past Georgia on the heath. To her horror, she realised Will was slumped awkwardly against the old bales, almost hidden by hay, and his eyes were closed. Immediately, Georgia could tell that Will was only just conscious. He needed help, and fast!

Reaching into her jacket pocket, adrenalin surged through Georgia. Hurriedly, she rang 999. She had never done this before, and felt a bit shaky, not knowing what she was meant to say.

"Police, fire or ambulance?" A kindly-sounding woman spoke on the end of the phone. Georgia tried to remain calm as she answered, thinking fast.

"Ambulance … and police as well!" Explaining the situation as clearly as she could, she told the woman that it concerned a missing boy and pony. Once the call operator had taken details, and promised an emergency vehicle, Georgia then rang Melanie – who answered hurriedly before the first ring had even finished.

"Georgia?" she said in an anxious voice. With a rush of guilt, Georgia realised that she had set off on her hack quite a while ago and that Melanie had probably started worrying about where she was too.

"Oh, Mel, I'm fine, but there's no time to explain!" Georgia said. "You need to come over to Will's old house as soon as possible. He's in trouble!"

☆ ☆ ☆

The seconds seemed to drag by like hours. If only Georgia could get into the barn. Pulling at the old door again as hard as she could, she realised why she couldn't open it – there was a bolt high above her head on the inside. Will must have barricaded himself in. Maybe someone a lot taller than Georgia would have been able to reach the bolt, and undo it if they pulled the doors open a little, but there was no way she could – she was too short. Grimacing with frustration, Georgia stepped back. Lily, calm now that she had found her friend Santa, nudged her on the arm, as if to say, "Hey, I could help!"

Looking from Lily, to the barn and back again, Georgia suddenly had a brainwave. "Right, my beauty." Georgia patted Lily gently. This had to work, and Lily had to trust her as much as she needed to trust Lily. Positioning the little mare right next to the barn doors, the palomino seemed to sense what Georgia wanted. Quickly, Georgia climbed back into the saddle, and then, very carefully, she started to stand so that she could perch on Lily's back like a circus rider and reach the bolt. Being small and light, Georgia had good balance, but it was still very tricky. Gradually raising herself up to her full height, she teetered for just a moment, wavering, her knees trembling. It wouldn't do anyone any good if she fell now and hurt herself.

"Easy, girl." Georgia soothed the little mare, praying she wouldn't move – and Lily, listening to her young mistress, stood as still as a statue, flicking her ears back and forth. Hardly daring to breathe, Georgia just managed to reach a hand through the crack in the barn door to find the bolt. She pulled it across and pushed open the heavy doors. She was in!

Jumping down from the palomino, she led Lily into the barn and quickly tied her up next to Santa. Lily was pleased to see her friend, and the mares whickered a greeting to one another before snuffling noses, ears pricked and eyes shining. Georgia hurried over to Will and crouched down beside him. It looked as though he had been trying to get some hay down from the hatch above the stables and judging from the loose bales piled

140

next to him, some had fallen on top of him. He stirred and gave a small groan, his face pale and his forehead cold and clammy.

"Will, are you OK?"

To Georgia's horror, as he turned his head, she saw a deep cut above his right eye that was bleeding heavily. Looking around her and thinking desperately, Georgia suddenly remembered the first aid lecture at the Pony Club rally. She knew what to do! Tearing off her cotton scarf she folded it and pressed it against his forehead, trying to stem the bleeding. Will placed his hand over hers to keep the pressure on the cut, realising what she was doing. His hands were icy cold. He was only wearing a T-shirt underneath his thin riding jacket and the inside of the barn was like a freezer.

Taking off her own jacket, Georgia wrapped it around Will's shoulders, and again, remembering what she'd learned at the Pony Club rally, took care not to move him in case he was seriously injured.

"Thanks, Georgia," Will whispered weakly, his teeth chattering with cold.

✩ ✪ ✩

Georgia felt dizzy with relief when she heard the distant wail of sirens and the familiar sound of Melanie's 4x4 storming up the rutted path towards the barn. The vehicle screeched to a halt and she heard footsteps running across to the barn. Two figures appeared in the doorway. She recognised the man from his pictures – it was Will's older brother Jasper, the famous show rider!

There wasn't time to think, or even say hello. Melanie and Jasper were quickly followed by two paramedics who rushed in, carrying their bags of equipment. Georgia was only too happy to let the grown-ups take over and she sank to the floor in shock, her legs finally buckling underneath her. All the stress of Lily getting loose on the heath, and then finding Will in this state had been a bit much. She was aware of lots of activity around her – Will being taken into an ambulance, and Melanie wrapping another jacket around her shoulders, but she felt one step removed from it, as though she were watching a drama on the television. Lily nudged her hand, concerned for her mistress, and Georgia nuzzled her mare back, breathing in her sweet, reassuring scent.

The short journey back to Redgrove was quiet. Simon had followed Melanie with the horsebox and she and Georgia loaded a calm Santa and Lily, ready for the journey back. It would have been pitch black by now, if not for the bright white moon lighting up the old stone barn. Staring out of the window at a night sky studded with stars, Georgia couldn't help but think they might have just arrived at the Horse of the Year Show by now, ready to bed Lily down in preparation for her class tomorrow. She shook herself. Will and Santa were safe. She just hoped Will would be OK. Not just after his accident, but when he found out that Santa had already been sold.

As if reading her thoughts, Melanie turned to her and smiled. "You did a very brave thing, you know, Georgia," she said kindly. "The paramedics said that if you hadn't found Will, it could have been far worse, especially on a freezing night like tonight. Poor boy, how unlucky life has been for him recently."

Georgia nodded sadly. She may not have got off to the best start with Will but now she understood why he was the way he was. He was desperately trying to live up to his brother's reputation, trying to save their livelihood. She hoped things would turn out OK for him

144

eventually, now that Jasper appeared to have lost the sponsorship deal for good.

"Georgia, are you OK?" Melanie cried.

Georgia gave a start and shook her head in confusion. She realised she must have dozed off mid-thought.

Nodding, she reassured Melanie she was fine, just exhausted. Right now, she felt sure that, given the opportunity, she would sleep for a week...

CHAPTER FOURTEEN

But the next morning, Georgia woke up early, as usual. It was still dark outside and completely silent. For a minute she wondered if the previous day's events had all been a dream. Then she realised she was still wearing her clothes from the night before! Her mum had sent her straight up to bed after taking one look at her, and she was so tired she'd just fallen into bed. Melanie had called Georgia's mum to let her know what had happened, but Georgia knew she would still be full of questions about Will's disappearance.

Creeping down the corridor, pausing to stroke Pip, who thumped her tail and blinked up at her, she let herself into the bathroom. After a quick shower, she pulled on her jeans and a warm fleece. She had a burning desire to go and visit Lily before school, realising with a start that she had no excuse not to go to school today as she wasn't at the Show.

Grabbing a banana from the fruit bowl and pausing to scribble a note for her mum, who was still asleep, Georgia slipped out of the front door. The cold October air took her breath away. There was a frost on the ground and the sky was clear, a weak sun just appearing to the east. It was going to be another perfect autumn day. The roads to Redgrove were quiet and she reached the yard in no time at all.

Lily whickered a familiar greeting, throwing her head up and down, as if to ask for her breakfast. To her relief, Santa's kind face also popped over the neighbouring door and she also whickered a low greeting.

Walking to the tack room, Georgia frowned. That was strange – the lights were already on. But it couldn't be Will in there, could it? To her surprise, Melanie's daughter, Sophie, clad in a dark-green cashmere jumper, her blonde hair piled messily on top of her head, was in the tack room, cleaning Lily's saddle.

She looked up and smiled when she saw Georgia. "Hey, G!" she said cheerfully, swigging from a mug of tea and rubbing a bit of soap into the soft brown leather at the same time. "So glad you're here. Mum was going to collect you if you didn't turn up, but we had a feeling that you might just come and visit Lily." Georgia must have looked confused, because Sophie chuckled. "Still ready to ride?"

"What ... what do you mean?" Georgia was totally bewildered now.

Sophie laughed again. "Horse of the Year Show, silly! We can still go!"

Georgia stared at her. "But we can't, we missed the stabling and the warm-up slots! There's no way we can go, is there?"

"Well, no, not if you just stand there gaping at me, we can't!" Sophie said, smiling widely. "Your class isn't until tonight, right? It's only a couple of hours away in the horsebox. Lily trusts you so much, she will be fine without a settling-in period. So, are you up for it?"

Sophie was so enthusiastic that suddenly a small thrill of excitement crept through Georgia. She realised that she didn't even feel nervous. What had recently seemed so impossible suddenly seemed within reach!

Melanie appeared in the door of the tack room, clutching her own mug of tea. Georgia noticed she was smartly dressed, in a tweed overcoat and long brown boots. "So what do you think, Georgia?" she asked, smiling. Drawing Georgia to one side, she placed a hand on her shoulder. "You really don't have to," she said softly, just to her. "I spoke to Janey and she told me how nervous you were when she taught you. I'm so sorry that I hadn't realised how you were feeling. You know, if you just relax and enjoy it and treat it as any other show, you and Lily would stand a real chance. You've worked so hard on her; it would be such a shame to miss this opportunity. But it's your choice, of course."

Suddenly, Georgia couldn't think of anything she would rather be doing. It wouldn't even matter if she came last, or fell off, they would still take Lily home at the end of the day, and Melanie and her friends would always be there to make her feel better. Slowly, the small bubble of excitement began to build until she was grinning as widely as Sophie.

"Sure!" she said, and this time she really meant it. But there was still something she had to check.

"What about Will? Is he OK?" she asked.

Melanie smiled. "Will is going to be fine," she said, reassuring Georgia. "I'll fill you in on the way there, but I promise you, he's doing great. The hospital took good care of him." She gestured towards the house before continuing. "He's fast asleep upstairs at the moment. We had a good chat last night, when he got home all patched up. Now, by my reckoning, we need to leave in a couple of hours at the latest. So we should get moving, and quickly! What do you reckon, Georgia? Up for the challenge?"

Georgia grinned. She really was. "Let's do it!" she said confidently.

"Hurrah!" Sophie cried, high-fiving Georgia with a saddle-soap-covered hand, and jumping up and down.

From that moment on, the yard was a whirl of activity. Sophie finished off Lily's tack and Georgia set to work giving Lily a warm bath, conditioning her creamy mane and tail before rugging her up in her lucky white cotton sheet. Emma joined them at the yard with Georgia's mum, who brought along her daughter's bag of show gear, which had been packed weeks ago. There was an excited buzz as Melanie handed around a tray of tea and bacon sandwiches, ready for the journey.

Georgia looked around her before climbing into the lorry cab. She couldn't help but feel that someone very important was missing, and it just

the PALOMINO PONY

wasn't the same. Just then, her stomach flipped at the familiar, welcome sight of Dan strolling through the yard gates, his crooked grin firmly in place, looking handsome in a navy jumper and waxed coat.

"Dan!" Georgia gasped, wondering if she was seeing things. "You came!"

"I texted him, silly, told him about all the drama last night." Emma nudged her friend. "You two are made for each other, and I didn't think you would ride as well without him!"

Georgia flushed, looking up at her other best friend, who was smiling down at her warmly, his face still tanned and freckly due to long days spent outside. "Dan, I—" she began.

Dan smiled and put a finger to her lips. "Shhh, Georgia. We'll talk after your class."

Emma was going to go in the car with Georgia's mum, and Dan and Sophie would accompany

153

Georgia in the lorry. Georgia was so grateful that Dan was there with her. It felt right with him sitting up besides her, like they were just off to the local Pony Club show and not one of the biggest championships in the equestrian world!

CHAPTER FIFTEEN

As Redgrove village slipped past and the winding country roads turned into the motorway that would lead them towards the showground, Melanie briefly explained that Will had been taken to hospital by ambulance the night before, and that Jasper had gone with him. He had been let out later on that evening, having been given a clean bill of health – apart from his forehead, which had needed stitching, and strict instructions to take it easy. Melanie had picked them both up, along with Sophie, who was instantly smitten with Jasper. They were staying at Redgrove Farm for the day while they found their feet. Santa was safe in her stable with Wilson and Callie for now.

"I'm sure they'll explain more later," Melanie said, turning to Georgia with a smile, "but Will was quite determined that you should ride today." She gestured towards the glove box. "Here," she said. "Look in there. Will wrote you a note when he was let out of hospital last night."

Intrigued, Georgia opened the glove box and, sitting on top of Sophie's old rosettes and show schedules was a torn-out page from a notebook. Will's scrawled handwriting filled the page. "Go for it, Georgia!" the note read. "Just enjoy your Barbie pony and feel lucky that she's yours. You can do it!"

Georgia folded the paper and tucked it into her pocket, feeling a lump in her throat. She was desperately sad for Will, who had lost Santa. She would put the note inside the pocket of her tweed coat later on, for luck. Dan placed a hand over hers, and she started to feel the familiar flutters of excitement that she did before every show. She was going to ride like she meant it tonight, for Will, for Santa and for Lily!

✿ ✪ ✿

The Horse of the Year Show was held in the huge international centre on the outskirts of Birmingham, and for Georgia it felt strange to drive past city tower blocks and motorway bridges so close to a show instead of the usual green fields and farmland. However, as they turned into the lorry park, the familiar sight of hundreds of gleaming shiny horseboxes met them. Security guards signed them in, and Melanie carefully brought the horsebox to a stop at the end of a row. They had arrived! Melanie was all business as she swung down from the cab, off to enquire if they could still use Lily's booked stable to settle her in a bit before the class.

Georgia peeked into the horse section of the lorry. Lily was calmly surveying the scene through the window, tearing off mouthfuls of hay from her net. She really had never looked better.

Then Melanie was back and she gave Georgia a big thumbs-up. "Stables OK," she reported.

Georgia swung the ramp down and gently unloaded the little mare, leading her towards the large stabled area on the designated concrete pathway. The lorry park was buzzing with excitement, as riders milled around, jackets over their tweed to keep out the October chill, hands clutching paper cups of tea and coffee. This was really happening; she was going to ride at the

Horse of the Year Show!

The stabled area was alive with activity and riders were busy warming up their ponies for the classes before Lily's. Pretty Dartmoors, Exmoors and Shetlands cantered figures of eight and practised extended trots across the diagonals, their riders wearing cream jodhpurs, the younger ones sporting brightly coloured ribbons in their hair. Grooms, parents and trainers milled around, chattering excitedly among themselves. Dan joined Georgia as she unbandaged Lily, and settled her in with her new hay net. He was carrying a rucksack in his hand and had a big grin on his face.

"What's up?" Georgia asked as Dan produced a flat cap and a tweed waistcoat from his bag.

"I'm going to be your groom," Dan said, his smile growing even wider.

Georgia knew instantly what he meant. Riders

159

needed one of their team to come into the ring once the ponies were lined up, to help them unsaddle the ponies ready for inspection.

Normally, Melanie did this. Dan must have asked if he could take her place. Georgia felt a warm glow in her tummy – she was going to have Dan in the ring with her during the biggest class of her life. He was so good to her, even after everything.

"That's brilliant!" Georgia flung her arms around him, before she could stop herself.

Dan looked both pleased and embarrassed as Georgia flushed scarlet, realising what she had done. To cover his own blushes, Dan placed the flat cap on his head and gave a little nod. "So – what do you think?"

"You look the best," Georgia said happily. "The very best!"

CHAPTER SIXTEEN

Soon it was time to get Lily tacked up so that Georgia could warm up in the crowded sand arena adjacent to the stables. She had missed the early morning warm-up, which would have allowed her to ride into the arena and get used to everything, so she was just going to have to cross her fingers and hope Lily didn't spook too much.

The little mare stood quietly as everyone fussed around her. Melanie adjusted her saddle for the umpteenth time, Georgia gave her bridle another wipe and Sophie gave Lily's pale-blonde tail one final brush. Emma milled around, making Georgia smile as she pointed out familiar ponies and riders. Dan adjusted his outfit. He really did look the part. Georgia checked again to make sure that her lucky tie pin was firmly fixed to her tie and that Will's letter was tucked into her pocket.

The other riders in Georgia's class were already starting to warm up. Their pretty Welsh ponies were a myriad of colours – roans, bays, greys and a couple more palominos, although lighter in shade than Lily. Riders turned in half-recognition as Georgia started to walk Lily around the edge of the arena, patting her and talking softly to keep her calm.

The atmosphere was charged and Lily seemed to

pick up on it, quivering slightly in anticipation. Her delicate ears flicked back and forth, concentrating on Georgia's voice. Remembering how badly she had ridden during her last lesson with Janey, Georgia felt herself tense just for a moment, as she eased Lily into a trot. Then, remembering Will's note folded in her jacket pocket, she took a deep breath. It didn't matter what happened. She was going to ride Lily well to show the palomino how much she meant to Georgia.

All too soon, Georgia found herself standing in the collecting area outside the ring where her class was being held. She had seen a glimpse of the arena as the walkway cleared. It was vast, and surrounded by hundreds of spectators, including her mum, who was nervously clutching the show programme as she waited for Georgia's entrance into the ring. And then, drawing in her breath, she and Lily danced through the gates and into the sand arena. There was no doubt about it, Lily stood out from the crowd. All of the Welsh ponies moved beautifully, and all were deserving of a place at the Horse of the Year Show, but Lily was something special.

Like all shows, the class consisted of a group trot and canter. Several ponies were over-excited by the atmosphere, and Georgia held her breath as they darted and spooked to the side. It didn't upset Lily, and soon they were standing waiting for the individual show, and the part that Georgia had been dreading. All the sleepless nights, all of the disastrous schooling sessions, had been leading up to this. As they waited in line for their turn, Georgia thought about everything that had happened during the last month, and patted the pocket that contained Will's note.

She thought about where she was happiest riding Lily, and pictured the bottom meadow, cantering up the hedge line, or riding over the hills between Redgrove Farm and Dan's farm and meandering back up the sunlit lane towards the yard. Georgia loved competing Lily, and adored shows. But she had allowed the event to take over her true enjoyment of riding. Will losing his beloved pony, and Georgia's ride to rescue him, had opened her eyes and reminded her how precious this chance was. She became so lost in her thoughts that she nearly didn't hear the steward call her forwards!

Just in time, Georgia nudged Lily on and greeted the judge with a polite good evening and a big smile. Touching his cap towards her, the judge indicated that she should start. Squeezing Lily's sides and urging her on into her trademark floating trot, Georgia couldn't help but grin. They were at the Horse of the Year Show! All the spectators, all the ponies, even the judge melted away as Georgia and Lily danced through their individual show.

Trotting across the diagonal, Lily extending her long legs like a world-class dressage horse, Georgia froze. This was her weak spot. Feeling her nerves, Lily flicked an ear back, her trot becoming slower, feeling unsure as she waited for Georgia to guide her. It felt as though water was rushing through Georgia's ears, her breathing becoming ragged. Time seemed to stand still. Taking a huge gulp of air, closing her eyes for a second, Georgia again tried to picture Lily cantering in the bottom meadow, then she picked up again.

She would lose precious marks for showing that moment of hesitation but it didn't matter. Georgia had overcome her nerves and as they flew down the long side in a gallop, she could almost laugh with relief.

There was just the confirmation section to go now. Georgia could have burst with pride as Dan joined her in the ring, carrying the wicker basket of brushes and cloths like a true professional. Deftly, he unsaddled Lily and gave her a quick polish so that Georgia could trot her up in hand in front of the second judge. Dan winked at her as he departed, mouthing, "You were brilliant," and she felt her heart leap.

Once Georgia had remounted and walked back into line, she felt a huge sense of relief. It really didn't matter what happened now. She had just achieved one of her biggest dreams – riding at the Horse of the Year Show. And they would take Lily home afterwards in the horsebox, and stop for hot chocolate, like they always did after a competition.

And after that – well, she would have a half-term holiday and then they would have cold crisp winter rides to look forward to, indoor showjump rallies, maybe even the Pony Club Mock Hunt.

Lily was hers to ride forever, and that meant more than any rosette.

Georgia was so busy planning all of this in her mind that she didn't notice the buzz among the competitors at first. The two judges were taking an awfully long time, looking at their mark sheets, huddled together. Eventually, one of them stepped forwards, and tipped his bowler hat at Georgia and a boy on a gorgeous bay stallion. Georgia's stomach did a triple somersault. Both competitors nudged their ponies out of the line-up, exchanging curious glances.

The judge explained that they were on equal marks in first place. "But we have to follow the rules," he said, looking down at his sheet. "And the highest ride mark wins, and that goes to … 154."

There were whoops and cheers from a section of the crowd as the boy on his bay stallion grinned from ear to ear, punching the air with delight.

Georgia had come second … but she was elated! She knew the hesitation in her show had cost her the marks. But she was far from upset. It was just something to work on for the future. Her little Lily – a rescue pony who they'd found bedraggled and lost on a wet mountainside – had just come second at the biggest horse show in the country! Georgia felt her heart swell with pride as the judge presented her with her beautiful rosettes, including one for best mare.

"And I had better tell you," he said in a kindly voice, removing his bowler hat. "Your confirmation mark was the highest of the day. You have a pony with real star quality, young lady. Well done."

Georgia could have fainted with pride! The lap of honour was a teary blur, the rosettes streaming through Lily's mane as the proud palomino revelled in the moment and lapped up the crowd's adoration.

Chapter Seventeen

As Georgia hugged Lily over and over, the evening's events began to sink in. She rugged up the little palomino and, still feeling dazed, settled her back into her temporary stable. People were congratulating her left, right and centre, but Georgia couldn't quite take it in yet – her head was still spinning.

"That's Ellen Whittaker!" Emma clapped her

hand over her mouth, giggling, as a pretty blonde girl in a flashy red jacket paused to pat Lily and chat to Georgia. Dan just couldn't stop grinning.

Everyone was in a party mood – Sophie danced around with Melanie and stuffed Lily full of carrots at the same time. Even Janey, who was normally brisk and firm, was teary-eyed and lost for words. Georgia was thrilled to see Josephine Smalley and her daughter, Alice, who had been competing in the show hunter pony class.

Just then, other riders turned to gawp as two familiar faces joined the celebrations. It was Will and his older brother Jasper. Georgia half expected Jasper to be dressed in breeches and shiny black boots, like his photographs, but he looked quite normal in jeans and a checked shirt. He certainly had charisma though, and she suddenly felt quite shy.

However, she was delighted to see her friend

Will looking back to normal other than the stitches above his right eye.

"Will!" she exclaimed, wondering how he was going to be after the dramatic events of the last few days. She needn't have worried – Will instantly gave her a huge hug, swinging her round and grinning.

"Hey, Georgia," he said warmly. There was no trace of arrogance and no awkwardness in his voice.

"How is, I mean, how are you ... how ... what about Santa?" Georgia didn't know where to start.

Will laughed. "Well, first I'd better thank you for saving me ... the doctors said that if you hadn't showed up when you did..." For a minute the smile faded, and he looked totally vulnerable.

"It was all Lily," Georgia broke in, running her hand gently over the little palomino's ears, who leaned in to her as she spoke. "One thing I've been wondering about, though – how did she know to head towards your old house?"

Will patted Lily's neck as he explained. "You know when Mel asked me to ride Santa and lead Lily?"

Georgia thought back and remembered the day that she and Melanie had gone to the saddler together. She nodded.

"Well, I rode that way," Will continued, looking thoughtful. "To visit the cottage where my brother and I grew up. I thought I would check it out, just in case I needed…" He paused.

"To get away from everything?" Georgia said gently.

"Well, not exactly," Will said with a rueful smile. "But then I heard from Jasper – the night we had the fish and chips in the tack room – that we had definitely lost the sponsorship. Even though Melanie told me everything would be OK, I didn't know if it would be. It was certain that Santa would go and I just couldn't stand the thought of her being sold. So I left in a hurry, but only to hide her. I knew Ryan wouldn't waste any time picking her up, so I thought if I moved her from Redgrove, it would buy me some time…"

He paused again. "I was trying to settle her in, then I slipped getting down some hay. I was rushing, panicking…" He turned to his brother, looking slightly unsure, and Jasper cleared his throat.

"It's my fault," Jasper said, placing a hand on his brother's shoulder. "I shouldn't have put all that pressure on you. The loss of the yard, and our sponsorship, that's my responsibility, not yours."

"But what will you do now?" Georgia couldn't help but ask. "And what about Santa? Oh, Will – you love her so much."

"It's all OK, Georgia." Will grinned. "It's going

174

to be fine. Just ask Melanie!"

Georgia turned around to look at Melanie, who was smiling happily.

"I bought Santa back," she said. "Not for me, of course! Will and Jasper are going to pay me back when they can, a bit at a time." She stroked Lily. "When I heard that Santa had been with the boys for over ten years, I couldn't bear the thought that she might end up somewhere horrible. She's an old girl who deserves a good retirement after all the prizes she's won for them *and* their sponsors."

For a moment, Georgia was speechless, and then she gave Melanie a huge hug. Melanie was so kind and always thought about the ponies first. "Wow," she said, totally in awe of her. "You really are the best, Mel!"

Melanie chuckled. "I could see how Will loved Santa – just like you love Lily, and then I thought about Wilson and Callie... I know that I want to keep them forever after all they've done for me. Santa deserved that as well."

Georgia turned to Will and Jasper. "So what will you do now?"

Smiling, Will turned to his older brother. "Can I tell them, Jasper?" he said.

"Of course," his brother said. "It's going to be public knowledge soon enough anyway."

Turning back to Georgia, Will smiled. "We're moving back to Redgrove," he said happily.

"So you've lost the yard?" Georgia blurted out before she could stop herself.

"Yes," Jasper said, in a regretful voice. "All those years of hard work, riding some of the best ponies money could buy, and now nothing. Just one pony left, but, without doubt, the most loyal pony I've ever ridden."

Then, smiling, he explained that Janey had heard about their predicament and had offered him a teaching position within the Pony Club. They needed someone young and vibrant, and Jasper was a hero among his old club. He also had a couple of young ponies lined up that he was going to bring on for their owners, and earn a small salary.

"But where will you live?" Georgia asked.

Will grinned happily. "Back at our old house!" he said in an excited voice. "It never sold and so Mum has agreed to rent it to Jasper – for just a small amount at first, until he finds his feet."

Pausing, his smile grew even wider. "And even better, I'm going to go back to school – your school! Now we're not always showing and jumping, Jasper doesn't have to home-school me any more. And I can still do shows with Santa, if I want. She'll do brilliantly in the veteran classes." He took a deep breath. "I can't thank you enough, Melanie."

Melanie just smiled. Georgia thought she couldn't admire her any more than she did at that very moment – first, helping her rescue Lily, and now ensuring that Santa's future was safe. She decided that if she didn't make it as a famous show rider, or a veterinary nurse, she would be perfectly happy owning a yard like Melanie and helping ponies in need. In fact, maybe she could do both, or all three. After all, Lily had been a rescue pony and now she had won second place – technically joint-first! – at the most prestigious horse show in the country. At that moment, her thoughts were interrupted by a familiar cry, as her mum pushed her way through the crowds and into the stable area.

Flinging her arms around her daughter, she wiped tears from her cheeks as she congratulated her over and over again.

"Thanks, Mum." Georgia hugged her mum

back, clinging to her for just a few seconds. "And sorry I've not been myself recently – everything was getting to me…" Her voice trailed off.

"I know, darling." Mrs Black smiled at her daughter. "And next time you need to tell someone!"

"I will, Mum, I promise," Georgia said solemnly.

Lily nudged her at that point, as if to say "Hey!" and Georgia chuckled, putting her arms around the little mare's elegant neck. "And you can have a holiday now!" she said, hugging the beautiful palomino all over again.

☆ ☆ ☆

Georgia's phone was beeping madly with text messages from her friends at school and even from Harry and Lottie and the other Pony Club members – good news travelled fast. With everyone still buoyed up by the celebrations, and the stable for Lily booked for the night, Melanie suggested pizza at a nearby restaurant to carry on the party.

Dan, Emma and Sophie whooped and cheered. Will and Jasper would join them as well, and Janey, too. Georgia had a funny feeling Will would become a good friend of the group now that he was moving back to the area for good.

A night celebrating with her friends and her mum would be amazing but first Georgia just wanted a few minutes alone with Lily, to thank her. As everyone drifted off to get ready for supper, Georgia slipped into Lily's stable and placed her arms around her neck. The little mare stood quietly, enjoying the attention.

"I promise I will never let my nerves get to me again," she whispered into her ear.

Now they had finished the Show, she felt as though she could do anything with Lily. Maybe they would qualify for the Horse of the Year Show next year, and who knew what would happen then!

Georgia thought about what she had said to her careers adviser. She decided that she definitely did want to have her own yard, but only with ponies that needed rescuing, like Lily. She felt a moment of pride at how far Lily had come. She knew Lily trusted her more than anyone, and it was the best feeling in the world.

Looking up, she saw Dan leaning over the stable door, smiling and wearing her rosettes like earrings. Georgia laughed. "Hey," she said, slightly shyly.

"You were brilliant, Georgia," Dan said warmly.

"I'm so sorry I couldn't tell you how nervous I was," Georgia stammered.

"That's OK," Dan smiled. "Tell you the truth, I was a bit worried you fancied Will, and that's why you were being so off with me. I thought you secretly liked him…" His voice trailed off and he looked a bit embarrassed, as Georgia laughed in amazement.

"No way!" she said sincerely. "I never thought of him like *that*! It was only that I knew you could tell how nervous I was, but I just didn't want to face up to it, and … oh … well…" she stammered, as Dan grinned.

"Friends again?" he said.

"Always!" Georgia cried, then chuckled as she gestured for Dan to look at Emma, who was giggling and flirting with Will over by the entrance to the stables. They both laughed.

"Now, that looks like trouble!" Dan said in amusement, and then softened as he turned back to Georgia. "Ready to celebrate?"

"Sure," Georgia grinned, gathering up her jacket and hat, but reluctant to stop hugging her beautiful little mare. "Wish she could come as well!" she said.

"Tell you what," Dan said. "Let's go and have pizza with everyone, then come back and see Lily – just you and me." Taking her hand, he led Georgia out of the stable and she glanced back at the palomino, who gazed at her with her soulful amber eyes.

Dan was right. Georgia would go and celebrate with all the people who had helped her get this far, and then come back for a goodnight cuddle with her pony, who was the bravest and sweetest creature Georgia had ever known.

And then they would drive home to Redgrove where Wilson and Callie and Santa would be waiting. They had crisp winter rides, rallies and shows to look forward to, and Lily was hers, now and for always.

And nothing would ever be more important than that!

ACKNOWLEDGEMENTS

Nosy Crow would like to thank Katy Marriott Payne for letting her lovely palomino pony star on the covers of this series.

If you liked this, you'll love

EMILY'S DREAM

by

HOLLY WEBB

Turn the page for a sneak peek!

ONE

"Shove up a bit." Emily squished herself on to the bench between Maya and the arm. "Oooh, it's cold. I thought this was supposed to be the summer term? I wish I'd brought my gloves."

Poppy nodded. "I know. I took Billy for a walk down by the canal yesterday after school and I nearly froze."

"Is it looking OK?" Izzy asked anxiously. "I haven't been down there for weeks."

"There was a tiny bit of litter – it's OK, Iz, I picked it up! – but no one had dumped anything. And the mural under the bridge still looks great, Poppy."

The four girls had organised a clean-up weekend down by the canal, after Poppy and Izzy had taken Billy down there and he'd got caught up in an old bicycle that someone had thrown into the water. They'd even been on the radio, appealing for people

to come and help.

"How could you be cold when you were out with Billy?" Maya asked, nudging Poppy. "He goes so fast, you must have been running to catch up with him."

"I know!" Poppy shivered. "So just think how cold I would have been on my own."

Emily suddenly let out a massive sigh, and the others wriggled round to look at her in surprise.

"What's the matter?" Maya asked, and Emily shrugged.

"Sorry. It was just hearing Poppy talk about Billy. You're so lucky having him. He's gorgeous."

Poppy sniffed. "Some of the time he is."

Izzy giggled. "What did he do?"

"Only ruined one of my sketchbooks," Poppy said grumpily. "I still love him, but it was a close thing for five minutes there."

"How? What happened?" Maya asked, trying not to grin. Billy was a very accident-prone bull terrier, and he always seemed to mix Poppy up in his mess too.

Poppy rolled her eyes. "I was sitting at the kitchen table, just doodling a bit, and I had a couple of biscuits..."

"I get the feeling I know where this is going." Izzy

wrinkled her nose.

"Exactly." Poppy sighed. "Well, I wasn't thinking – it was the drawing, it was really nice, and I sort of forgot, and I left the biscuits at the edge of the table. Billy sniffed them out – he's got a nose like a bloodhound, for food anyway. We could use him to track biscuit thieves, no problem."

"So he ate your biscuits," Emily said, frowning. "I don't see what that's got to do with the sketchbook. Unless he thought that was a biscuit too." Billy was well known for being a bit stupid. Poppy's brothers called him the dumb blond.

"He *didn't* eat the biscuits." Poppy shook her head. "He tried to. But he missed when he jumped up, and he thumped his head on the underneath of the table."

"Oh no! Was he all right?" Emily gasped.

Poppy smiled at her reassuringly. "He was fine. He's got a skull made of wood, Dad says. He was just a bit confused about where his biscuits had gone. But he shook the table up – almost tipped it over. You know how strong he is. And the vase of flowers fell over, and spilled water all across my sketchbook. And me."

"I wouldn't mind. I'd still love a dog like Billy," Emily

said, staring into the distance. She was dreaming about her ideal dog, the others could tell. "Or a cat. A big soft furry one, with a tail like a scarf… Or even a hamster. Well – maybe I wouldn't like a hamster so much, you can't really cuddle a hamster. But any sort of pet would be nice…"

"Jake and Alex have got a friend who wants to sell his pet tarantula," Poppy said brightly.

Emily glared at her. "Any sort of pet *with fur*," she added.

"Oh, Sam says it's *very* furry. And affectionate," Poppy promised her. "It likes to sit on your shoulder."

Emily shuddered. "You know what I mean!"

"Your mum and dad won't let you have a pet at all?" Maya asked sympathetically. She had a huge black cat called Henry, who liked to curl up next to her when she was doing her homework. He was Maya's mum's cat really, but she was off touring or filming so much of the time that he had adopted Maya instead.

"No." Emily shook her head. "I think Dad would quite like to have a dog, but Mum says she would be the one who ended up having to look after it, while he was at work, and we were all at school. She reckons she's got quite enough people to look after, with me and Toby and James and Sukie. And when I tried to explain about it being different, and wanting something to curl up with, she said I was welcome to curl up with Sukie, especially when Sukie woke up at two o'clock in the morning." She slumped down a little on the bench, sighing disgustedly. "And she says if I want to take something for a walk, that's not a problem either, I can just put Sukie in the pushchair."

"Isn't it nice having a little sister?" Maya asked, frowning a little. She was an only child, and quite fancied having someone else around to play with. "You could dress her up. It would be fun…"

Emily stared at her. "You have no idea! Sukie won't wear anything except her wellies. And I mean *just* her wellies. It's a complete battle getting her to wear anything else. She'd rather live in a nappy, her wellies and maybe a woolly hat if she feels a bit cold. I'd love to see you trying to dress her up." Emily snorted with laughter. "She'd probably bite you."

"Oh…" Maya sounded rather downcast. It wasn't what she'd imagined at all.

"I can sort of see your mum's point, though," Izzy said quietly. "There's an awful lot of you in your house already. Have you got room for a dog?"

"A small one…" Emily held out her hands, just a

little way apart. "A nice little dog…"

Poppy nodded. "You'd just have to make sure it was really well trained. Not like Billy," she added, before any of the others could say it for her. "Dad took him to lots of training classes, but he never really got the hang of it. You'd need a dog that was very small, and very sensible." She frowned. "I don't know what breed that would be."

Emily shook her head. "Me neither."

"Maybe your mum will let you have a dog when Sukie gets a bit bigger," Maya said, trying to be comforting, but Emily smiled at her lopsidedly.

"I know what she'll say then – that we're all a bit bigger, and there's even less room. I'll just have to keep visiting Billy."

"He can come and have a holiday with you if you like," Poppy volunteered, a bit too eagerly.

Emily giggled. "I don't think that would help convince Mum, would it?"

"Maybe not," Poppy agreed. "Unless you managed to find a really nice small well-behaved dog, and sort of compared it to Billy to make it look even more perfect."

"Yeah, that might work." Emily sighed. "Except I'll never get the chance to try it out."

They were all silent for a moment, thinking.

"Isn't there another way you could have a pet, without actually owning one?" Maya suggested slowly.

"Adopting a zoo animal, you mean?" Emily nodded. "I already have. I've got a snow leopard," she said, rather sadly. "Gran gave me him for my birthday. It's nice – I got a letter about him, and I've got a toy version of him on my bed. But it isn't the same. I've only ever seen him once, and then he was up at the top of his – well, it wasn't a cage. Sort of a big pen with trees and rocks. He wouldn't come down."

"I didn't quite mean that," Maya said. "It was what Poppy said about having Billy for a holiday. Couldn't you be a petsitter? I don't mean having the pets living at your house, but popping in to feed them and give them a cuddle while their owners are away. Or maybe you could take dogs for walks when their owners can't manage it?"

Emily stared at her. "Do you think people would let me?" she asked excitedly. "I mean, I love dogs, and I've got loads of dog books, but I've never actually owned one."

"I bet they would if they saw you with a dog,"

Poppy agreed. "You're brilliant with Billy. Anybody could see that you're a dog person." She smirked. "And other pets too, of course. Maybe Sam would like you to pop in and cuddle his tarantula while he goes on holiday." Then she dodged as Emily pretended to smack her.

"Seriously, I bet you could do that. You'd just need to find a way to let people know about you." Maya frowned. "And I suppose you'd really only be able to help out people in Appleby, wouldn't you? Unless your mum would let you go to any of the other villages on your bike."

"I don't think she would." Emily frowned. "She gets panicky about us being out on the roads on our bikes. Which is totally fair when you think about Toby and James, but not for me. But there are lots of people with dogs and cats round our village. Somebody must need a dog-walker."

"You know what else there is in Appleby?" Izzy put in, her pale-blue eyes round with excitement.

The others shook their heads, and Izzy beamed. "The shelter. You know," she added as they looked at her blankly. "The animal shelter! Ummm, it's called Appleby Animal Rescue, or something like that?"

"Oh! Yes, I forgot. But Mum isn't going to let

us adopt a pet from there, Izzy, even though I'd love to," Emily objected.

"I know, I don't mean that," said her friend. "Couldn't you go and help out?"

Emily looked at her blankly for a moment, then she squeaked with excitement. "Why didn't I ever think of that before? I know I'm always saying it, but you're a genius, Izzy!" She jumped up off the bench and hugged Izzy so hard that she squeaked too, and her nose went bright pink, the way it always did when she was pleased.

Emily perched herself on the arm of the bench, frowning thoughtfully. "Today's Thursday, and Toby's got judo after school, so I can't go tonight—"

"Your mum lets him do judo?" Poppy asked disbelievingly. "Like, so he's being *trained* how to fight people? Is that a good idea?"

Emily shrugged. "Apparently, it's supposed to help you calm down – by kicking things, I guess. Who knows. Anyway, we'll have to take him to the sports centre, so Mum'll be trying to cook dinner and everything in a rush. She won't be up for me disappearing off to the animal shelter. But I could definitely go tomorrow afternoon." She bounced excitedly. "Oh, I really hope they do need

some help. Even if it's just cleaning out guinea pig hutches or something."

"Will your mum let you do it?" Maya asked suddenly. "I mean, if she's not keen on dogs…"

Emily shook her head. "Oh no, that's the stupid thing. Mum loves dogs. She had a gorgeous Labrador when she was my age. But she says she hasn't got time to look after one properly now. I'm sure she'd be OK with me going to the shelter. Especially if it stops me moaning about having a dog of our own. Oh, I can't wait to go!"

TWO

"Emily, it's me! Maya. I couldn't wait until tomorrow. What did your mum say about helping out at the shelter?"

Maya knew right away how excited Emily was – her words were falling over each other, she was talking so quickly!

"She was fine – she said it was a great idea, and she knows how much I love dogs. Dad said it sounded brilliant, but I had to make sure I still had time for my homework if I go and help at the shelter, because I've already got dancing, but I told them it would be OK. Dancing's only on Mondays, I could help any other night for a bit, or maybe at the weekend."

"So you're definitely going to go and ask tomorrow?" Maya asked.

"Yee-ees," Emily agreed. "That's the only problem. What do I say to them? And what if they say no, they

don't want anybody?"

"Mmmm. I should think they'd need as much help as they can get," Maya said thoughtfully. "They'd be more likely to hug you and hand you a bag of dog food. You're not really nervous, are you?"

"A bit," Emily admitted. "It's just the thought of walking in and talking to someone I've never met before…"

Maya *hmmmed* for a moment. "Want me to come with you?" she suggested.

"Yes!" Emily yelped. "I mean, yes, please. Are you sure?"

"I'd like to. I've never been to an animal shelter," said Maya.

"Actually, me neither," Emily admitted. "I'm not sure what it's going to be like."

"Would your mum let you come back to my house tomorrow? You're on the bus on Fridays, aren't you? Then we could go to the shelter together. It's really close to mine."

"Hang on, I'll check."

Maya could hear discussion going on in the background, and what sounded like a full-on fight between Toby and James at the same time. She could see why Emily had said it would be too tricky to get to the shelter tonight. She should have rung later on, she thought to herself crossly. But she'd been so keen to know what Emily's mum and dad had said.

"Yes!" Emily said breathlessly into the phone.

"Sorry! I shouldn't have rung now, your mum's trying to do tea and everything."

Emily giggled. "No, it's fine. James squirted ketchup all over Toby while I was asking her, that's all. She was dithering a bit because she wanted to take me to the shelter so they could see she was OK with the idea, but now she says she'll write me a note, with her mobile number and everything. Then they can call her."

"OK. I'll check with Dad, but I know it'll be fine. He'll come with us, or maybe Anna will if he has to work."

"Is your mum away, then?" Emily asked. She and Poppy and Izzy couldn't help being a little bit curious about Maya's mum, who was a singer called India Kell. She didn't record as much any more, but she did a lot of TV work, and she was always flying off all over the place. (Which made Maya really cross. She was always trying to get her mum to use trains instead, but her mum said it wasn't really practical to get a train to the US, and a boat would take weeks.

She and Maya had agreed that she'd do carbon-offsetting and pay for trees to be planted instead. Maya's mum said this meant that somewhere there was a small forest that belonged to her, and she was planning to build a log cabin in it.)

"Mmmm, she's gone to some awards thing. She's presenting an award for Best New Act. I hadn't heard of any of the people who were up for it, and Mum said she wasn't sure she had either. But one of them had really nice hair, so she reckons he should win. Anyway, she won't be back until Monday."

"I know you don't like it when she's away, but you are lucky, you know…" Emily sighed. "Your dad's there most of the time, and Anna's the best cook. Do you think she'd make chocolate-chip cookies if we asked her really nicely?" Anna was Maya's family's housekeeper. She made gorgeous food, but she didn't approve of Maya being a vegetarian. She cooked lovely veggie stuff for her, but she knew how hard it was for Maya to resist bacon sandwiches, so she was always cooking them for Maya's dad, and wafting the delicious bacon smell all over the house.

"I bet she would. Especially if you ask her, Em. She likes you. She knows you help look after Toby and James and Sukie, and she says children should help out. She thinks I ought to have a little sister or brother, and then I wouldn't be spoilt rotten."

"But you aren't!" Emily told her in surprise. "That's why none of us could really believe it when you said you were India Kell's daughter. When you read about celeb kids, they've always got tiny sports cars, and pet zebras and things—"

Maya snorted with laughter.

"I'm serious! Or they've got half of Chelsea football team coming to help at their birthday party or something like that. You're normal. Well. Almost normal, anyway," Emily added sweetly. She was on the phone, so Maya couldn't slap her. "You do have your own laptop – which I'd kill for, by the way – and a mobile, and your house is enormous, but otherwise, you're not that different from me and Poppy and Izzy."

"I love you too," Maya said, still trying not to laugh. "Anyway. Tomorrow at mine, and I'll make Dad come with us. He could do with a walk."

"Do you think they'll say yes?" Emily asked anxiously, for about the fifth time since they'd set off.

"Yes!" Maya rolled her eyes.

"I think they'd be really glad of the help, Emily,"

Maya's dad put in. "The shelter's pretty tiny, and I'm sure I remember seeing an article about it in the paper – it's mostly run by one lady, and she's really overworked."

Appleby Animal Rescue was an old farmhouse, just outside Appleby village, where Emily and Maya both lived. It was a nice-looking house, not very big, but with a square yard in front of it, with stables and outhouses all round.

"Do you think all those building have got animals in them?" Emily asked, looking around in surprise. "I didn't think it would be this big."

"I suppose there isn't another animal shelter anywhere close," Maya said thoughtfully. "Any abandoned animals would have to come here." She nudged Emily. "So, are we going in?"